Dec'22

relye

SCI-FI FROM THE ROCK

A COLLECTION OF SHORT STORIES

SCI-FI FROM THE ROCK

EDITED BY ERIN VANCE & ELLEN CURTIS

BOOKS

Library and Archives Canada Cataloguing in Publication
    Sci-fi from the rock / edited by Erin Vance and Ellen Curtis.
ISBN 978-1-926903-29-3 (paperback)
    1. Science fiction, Canadian (English)--Newfoundland and
Labrador. 2. Fantasy fiction, Canadian (English)--Newfoundland
and Labrador. 3. Short stories, Canadian (English)--Newfoundland
and Labrador. 4. Canadian fiction (English)--21st century.
I. Curtis, Ellen, 1993-, editor II. Vance, Erin, editor

PS8329.5.N3S35 2016   C813'.087620806   C2016-900910-6
Second Edition ISBN: 978-1-989473-42-9
Copyright © 2016 Engen Books

Distributed by:
Engen Books
www.engenbooks.com
submissions@engenbooks.com

First mass market paperback printing: April 2016
Cover Image: Kyle Callahan Photography

Engen Books thanks Kyle Callahan Photography and Sci-Fi on the Rock for helping make
this collection possible.

THOUGHTS ON
SCI-FI FROM THE ROCK

"Melanie Collins was the last [story I] read and I wasn't disappointed. Melanie Collins has a wonderful way with words. Reading the stories makes me want to write again."

Jeremy Bulloch
Boba Fett

"Darren Hann can really write and he has an active imagination... he is inclined to include everything but the kitchen sink. I will definitely watch out for his prose in the future."

John Robert Colombo
Colombo & Company

"A wonderful testing ground for new authors. Not only do we get to see what stories work, but readers get an easily accessible venue to see what authors they enjoy following and might enjoy following in the future. The work of all three authors was fantastical and imaginative, each in their own special way."

Matthew LeDrew
author of *Black Womb* and *Infinity*

"[Steve Lake's] visit to the age-old conflict between vampires and werewolves is a good one, but too brief. I hope [he] will take this tale and develop it, hone it and publish a larger work with this story as an integral part."

Mark Vaughan-Jackson
The Telegram

CONTENTS

Foreword
Ellen Louise Curtis

When it first began in 2007, Sci-Fi on the Rock was the first convention of its kind to be held in Atlantic Canada for many years. I can still remember attending the first year, when the convention found itself crammed inside the Hotel Mount Pearl. I wore shiny silver sneakers, had purple hair, and excitedly dragged my mother to the event. These were the days when cosplay wasn't so widespread, and when my eccentric fashion choices were not the norm, even in the capital city.

My mother and my father had raised me on sci-fi and fantasy: on *Star Trek* re-runs, *Bladerunner*, *Labyrinth*, and *Star Wars*; on Anne McCaffrey and Mercedes Lackey novels; on bedtime stories about faeries and unicorns; and overall it was an experience I hadn't shared with my friends. This upbringing was how my mother got the responsibility of driving her quiet yet wild-eyed, excited daughter from the east end of St. John's all the way out to Mount Pearl. Back then, that seemed like a long way to go, and a lot of money to spend on gas.

Now, ten years later, people drive from across the province to attend Sci-Fi on the Rock. Heck, people are flying here from across the country to be part of this volunteer-run event. Some of my closest friends today are people I would have never met without Sci-Fi on the Rock. It's become an event that brings people of all walks of life, of many different nerdy interests, and of many talents, together.

By the second year, the event had grown immensely, to the point that it moved to the Holiday Inn in St. John's. That year, eagerly looking up the panel listings ahead of time, I decided to attend every writing related panel I could. I had been working on a manuscript for months, and I dreamed of it becoming more than just a pet project.

It was during Sci-Fi on the Rock II at one of these panels that I met Ken Tam and Matt LeDrew, each founders of their own publishing companies and authors themselves. I handed off my manuscript to Matt on a whim, wanting feedback and expecting the worst. The little research I had done into the industry had me absolutely terrified of receiving scathing rejection letters that would tear apart my work. Still, I wanted to grow. I wanted to be challenged.

Looking back now, I am utterly stunned that Matt enjoyed that manuscript. It hasn't seen the light of day since, and I've become more and more critical of my teenaged self's writing as the years have gone on. However, his encouragement early in my career made a world of difference to me. Sci-Fi on the Rock II became the moment I got my foot in the door and figured out what I wanted to do with my life: I wanted to keep writing.

The following year, Engen Books published *NewFoundSpecFic* as an imprint anthology. Now out of print, it was the first place I saw my name and my writing appear on a printed page. I was elated. That year, at Sci-Fi on the Rock III, I was behind a vendor table for the first time.

In 2010, working more closely with Matt, the first *Sci-Fi from the Rock* anthology was launched. It replaced *NewFoundSpecFic*, and was intended to celebrate the talent behind the Sci-Fi on the Rock convention. Convention organizers Darren Hann, Melanie Collins, and Steve Lake had their stories published in it. Two more editions were released in the years that followed, celebrating the talent that science fiction, fantasy, and horror authors from the Rock have to offer.

As the Engen publishing schedule grew wilder each year and our library of titles grew, Matt and I discussed going back to Engen's roots. A reflective blog post by Jaqui Tam, author of *Standing Tall: A Daughter's Gift*, and one of the first authors who attended Sci-Fi on the Rock, was one of many things that put the history of Sci-Fi on the Rock in focus for us. She wrote these words:

"[Iceberg Publishing] initially heard about Sci-Fi on the Rock from co-founder Darren Hann when we met at Polaris (then called Toronto Trek) in July 2006. He was planning the first Newfoundland convention for the following April, and was interested in having Kenneth participate as an author guest. We said yes, of course (I think it took a full half second of consideration), and when the time came we packed up books, banners, Iceberg wear and event supplies for a 40-hour whirlwind trip. We were able to go back again in 2008 and 2009, and had the pleasure of watching firsthand as the event flourished in terms of programming, guests, attendees, and profile. And every year it has gotten better.

We've met some great people because of Sci-Fi on the Rock, and have had the chance to make some special connections. I remember meeting Liz Durnford-LeDrew and her son Matt, who stopped by our table the first year to chat. Matt was a budding writer who was curious about publishing. By Sci-Fi on the Rock II, he was an author guest himself, set up at the table next to us with his new company Engen Books...

Sci-Fi on the Rock has given us great memories, lasting friendships, and loyal readers."

Many writers have attended and been created by the convention over the past ten years; and to commemorate that, this collection has been curated for the 10th anniversary of Sci-Fi on the Rock. Reaching out to former guests of the convention, attendees, and our previously published authors, my fellow editor, Erin Vance, and I have attempted to ensure that this collection encapsulates everything Sci-Fi on the Rock has brought to Newfoundland and Labrador. The stories that follow this forward are a mixture of some of the best talent connected to Sci-Fi on the Rock. In these pages you will find science fiction, fantasy, horror, and everything in between. My one hope is that you, the reader, will take as much joy from them as I have from the past ten years of Sci-Fi on the Rock.

With much love and wishing you happy reading,
Ellen Curtis
Editor

Kenneth Tam

Being raised by readers and writers, perhaps it was inevitable that Kenneth Tam would take up storytelling. Now one of Iceberg Publishing's partners and authors, he is responsible for more than thirty science fiction and alternate history novels, spread across four series.

Kenneth's early writing took place while he was completing his BA and MA in military history at Wilfrid Laurier University. During that time, he was awarded a Balsillie Fellowship from the Centre for International Governance Innovation in Waterloo, Ontario; and after that spent a year there working for Paul Heinbecker, Canada's former ambassador and permanent representative to the United Nations.

After his graduation, Kenneth joined the staff of Kitchener–Waterloo Member of Parliament Peter Braid, in the role of Communications Consultant. After those two years in the employ of the House of Commons, he spent four years working with his father as an advisor in wealth management, before moving to Edmonton, Alberta, and taking up the duties of Communications Coordinator with the Alberta Land Institute, at the University of Alberta.

Born in 1984 in St. John's, Newfoundland, Kenneth has also lived in Ontario and Alberta. Book events and convention appearances have taken him all across Canada, but like most Newfoundlanders, he finds his preferred travel destination is always home to the rock. That probably explains why the island — be it called Newfoundland or something else — turns up so often in his writing.

He presently lives in Edmonton, Alberta. The following excerpt serves as the prologue to his novel, *Whitecoat*, the first of many stories in the Champions series.

Whitecoat
Prologue

Hearing the water in her ears always helped Alex think. She figured she was a creature of the water — not that she had any particular right to be. Her body lacked the useful control surfaces that made fish and dolphins such natural swimmers, and she'd occasionally get rude reminders that she didn't have gills... but she still felt like a sea creature.

A strange, lanky, awkward, ocean-going mammal who did some of her best pondering while she floated in calm water, letting its soft sounds lap into her ears.

Of course, she was under no illusion that she was unique in this particular preference — many people found floating in their tub, or in a swimming pool, to be a peaceful experience. Some even enjoyed doing it in a pond, or a nice lake. Alex supposed some might even have attempted it in a slow-moving river, though she'd never been inclined to give that a try.

What did make her rather unique was the fact that her favourite place to float was slightly more dramatic than all those alternatives, and to be entirely fair, more dangerous too. For most people. But the air here was better, and the company far more interesting.

As she took a deep breath of the cool, moist air that was tickling as much of her skin as was above the surface, Alex Smith looked very slightly to her left. Nothing but open sky that way —— incredible blue sky looking down on an unusually placid, almost-painted ocean. There could be few more peaceful sights in either world, she imagined.

Then she tilted her head very slightly to the right and studied a great brown-green cliff towering over her. It was a sheer sheet of rock with crags, grasses and a few seagulls posted along it, all of them looking down at her with some confusion. What was a girl doing floating along a remote piece of the North Atlantic coast?

Well she was thinking. Obviously.

"Don't mind me," Alex called to her winged onlookers, though because her ears were in the water she couldn't quite hear her own voice. They mustn't have heard either, because none of them appeared to answer. Typical.

Beneath Alex the water was quite deep — she'd swum close to the cliff so she'd be out of the strong North Atlantic currents, and could lie back in peace, but the bottom was still a black mystery beneath her. There were probably fish down there, and they'd be wondering about her presence too... but those fellows had gills. Alex tended to limit her attempts at social conversation to creatures — human or otherwise — that inhaled oxygen from the air, instead of sucking it out of the water.

Not that her conversations ever got too far with the birds. She blamed her natural awkwardness, though that didn't stop her from trying. And today might be her last chance for a while.

The weeks ahead would be very busy ones — as much as she loved to disappear for day-long swims along the coasts of Newfoundland, her upcoming responsibilities probably wouldn't allow her much time for playing in the water. Today she'd have to get her fill...

And at least the weather was cooperating.

It was one of the most beautiful Augusts Alex had seen in her twenty years, and the North Atlantic water was somewhat less frigid than she was accustomed to. The temperature didn't bother her too much either way — one of the many benefits of her special physiology — but she imagined even ordinary people might have been able to wade out into the waves on a day like this. She wouldn't have recommended any of those people try to follow one of her lengthy swims — even on calm days, the currents of the North Atlantic were powerful — but perhaps some would have been able to float.

And yet nobody would have ever thought to try.

Alex was always alone in places like this — aside from the birds, and occasional sea creatures. A porpoise had once come through, but he'd been quite rude. The fish were similarly anti-social, so mostly she kept her own counsel. But that was fine — she had enough to think about.

Taking another deep breath of fine sea air, Alex closed her eyes and thought of her impending title — of what it would mean. It wasn't that the fate of the world would be exclusively in her hands... it was just that she'd be part of a large organization which could, on a given day, be responsible for the fate of the planet. Or, in fact, two planets. She was going to be a Champion.

No pressure.

There were thousands of Champions in the world, none older than twenty-five years. All of those who had preceded her were children of the savages, a breed of humans that had been taken to another planet by the decidedly unpleasant alien Hubrin, then genetically modified to be stronger, faster, and rather more cannibalistic.

Alex's parents had been part of an expedition to that planet — the Royal Newfoundland Regiment's mission that had discovered the Hubrin, defeated them, and made the world safe for colonization by the British Empire and the United States. They'd also freed the children of the savages — thousands of youths with these strengths, who had been saved from Hubrin hands in time to be able to grow up into civilized beings. With the passing of the Byng Policy in 1924, those talented children were destined to be Champions, and Alex was about to join their ranks.

But though she shared their strength and speed, she was different.

Unlike all other Champions she actually knew her real parents — they had raised her. She possessed Champion abilities because her mother Caralynne had been killed by the Hubrin, then brought back to life and rebuilt by their scientists to have savage strength and speed. That certainly made for an interesting story at the rare dinner parties Caralynne attended — *why yes, I was dead, and my insides were in fact put back together out of spare savage parts. Would you like to see my scar? No seriously, I'll show you my scar...*

Admittedly, part of Alex's self-proclaimed awkwardness might have come from the fact that her mother was often asked to leave fashionable society parties after she said such things (which was, of course, why she said them).

And Alex's father was no better. Caralynne had married an American drifter called Smith — a man who had mounted the rescue that sprung her from Hubrin captivity... even though he'd actually watched her die months before. Smith was wise and direct, but definitely not one for social situations. Alex hadn't even learned his first name until she was nine — he was always just 'dad' to her, and 'Smith' to everyone else.

So they were hopeless parents for teaching good social habits, and perfectly remarkable parents in just about every other way she could imagine. Smiling as she thought of them, Alex opened her eyes again.

She did not scream when she realized there was a seagull riding the breeze a few yards over her. Not at all. The technical term for her sound was a squawk, which is in fact a greeting in the seagull language.

Unfortunately, her dialect was wrong, because the seagull didn't seem to understand the noise. He just kept floating creepily above her, his stare far too intense. It was a look she'd occasionally seen before from unwanted admirers, so she knew she needed to dissuade him — but politely.

"Flattered by the attention, but... I'm here with someone. He's... a manatee. Which I will admit is unusual in these waters... he's visiting from the West Indies. He'll be right back, but he's just diving for seaweed..." she tried her excuse, but even as she was saying it, she knew her delivery wasn't convincing. Indeed, because she wasn't squawking, the gull probably didn't even understand.

The seagull proved he wasn't buying her story with

his very next move: he untucked his little legs and feet, then started flapping. It took Alex a second to realize what he was planning, and by the time she did it was too late: he touched down on her stomach.

The cheeky bastard. Admittedly, his gray feathers gave him a distinguished look, but this was far too forward. Landing on her? He hadn't even offered dinner... though considering how gulls transported meals, that was definitely for the best.

"I'm a cheap date, so don't share any food, okay?"

Hearing that, he squawked. Obviously this was the gull Casanova, and as he directed a smouldering stare down his beak at her, Alex had to admit it was nice to be pursued. Despite being twenty and quite eligible, she figured she was destined for spinsterdom; all Champions were required by the Byng Policy to marry ordinary people, so their genetic enhancements could be disseminated to the wider human race.

That seemed fine for the male Champions — ordinary socialite girls positively salivated at the chance to go with the dashing men who possessed special speed and strength. For female Champions, it was rather more complicated. While Alex's father hadn't been insecure about wedding a woman physically stronger than he, the hunt for a husband was undeniably more difficult for a girl who had the ability to lift her beau over her head one-handed.

And for Alex, the problem was especially acute: she was shorter and far less womanly than most of the Lady Champions. She certainly did not conform to the pinup standards in the magazines.

So maybe she should give this gull a chance. He could

fly — surely he wouldn't be insecure.

"There could be some logistical challenges, Mister Gull, but I'm open to talking about how this could work. Unless you already have kids. That's a deal-breaker."

He suddenly got quiet, and Alex realized her conditions were too stringent: of course he had kids. He was probably even married. That was it, Alex prepared to shoo off her admirer... but before she could, a dory appeared and did the job for her.

She frowned as soon as the boat drifted into view past her feet. How had she managed to miss the noise of its approach? Champions had exceptional hearing, and even in the water she should have been able to detect the sounds of fishing.

By now Mister Gull was spooked — probably worried he was about to be found out. His abrupt liftoff left Alex floating alone, watching as the dory eased right up alongside her.

At first she thought the silence meant the small craft was empty — if there were Newfoundland fisherman aboard, there'd have been more for her to hear. There also weren't any heads visible over the dory's high sides, so perhaps some poor man's lashings had come undone, and his livelihood had just drifted out to sea.

Alex could do something about that — and since her manatee suitor was depressingly fictional, it was clear she needed to get away from this seedy piece of coast before other gulls tried their luck. Torquing her body, she let her feet fall down from the surface so that she was vertical in the water, then began to kick, just her head remaining in the air.

Sounds got a bit sharper as the water cleared from her ears, and she caught a young voice sounding a panicked cry: "We's gonna hit the rocks!"

Aha, there were some boys on board, perhaps having gone out to drop a line in the water on this lovely day, but having lost control of their little boat. The Atlantic could be very unsympathetic in such situations — barely 400 miles from this very cliff, the same ocean had claimed the Titanic. But today was calm enough to give the young b'ys a chance, and of course, Alex was at hand.

Without pause, she swam up to the dory, closed her hands around its side, and pulled herself far enough out of the water to see who was aboard, "Sorry to interrupt..."

The resulting screams couldn't really be mistaken for squawks — two young boys were in the boat, and both of them had that same reaction to the arrival of a sea monster in their midst.

"Holy jumpin' Moses!" was the only intelligible string of sounds Alex managed to catch amongst a healthy outburst of expletives, and it made her smile.

"Nobody's called me Moses since I shaved my beard. Mind if I come aboard?"

Even with the Moses joke, she didn't get anything resembling a coherent answer. Probably her own fault. And now both boys looked like they were going to jump over the other side of the boat, which would have been a bad idea — in her experience, most fishermen couldn't swim. Realizing her terrible humor wasn't going to diffuse the situation, Alex sank back down into the water, then kicked hard and launched herself up into the air. She landed inside the boat like an eagle touching down; her feet planted easily on one of the thwarts running across the middle of the craft, then she lowered herself to a crouch before shifting to sit.

The boys both watched, jaws hanging slack.

"My jokes always sound funnier before I say them," she apologized with a smile. "What seems to be the trouble?"

She looked towards the bow of the boat first, and there the younger boy stared at her with wide eyes. Either the beard joke had been really terrible, or her landing had been over-dramatic, because he simply continued to stare at her in shock.

But he was only nine or ten, perhaps too young to quickly recover from bad humor. That in mind, Alex looked to the stern; the older boy there had to be teen-aged, and was probably the one in charge of this ill-fated expedition. But he wasn't answering either — possibly because he'd noticed that her French-made swimming costume did absolutely nothing to cover her legs.

"I'm going to have to piece this together on my own, aren't I?" Alex basically posed that question to herself, and the boy's eyes didn't budge. Great.

"You didn't tell me there was mermaids out here!"

Finally the younger one spoke from the bow, but his words were directed towards his brother. The elder boy still didn't manage to answer, so Alex looked back to the bow.

Holding up her hand in a wave, she tried once more, "Not a mermaid... though I was just pretending to date a manatee." That just earned her another confused look, so she gave up with a sigh: "I'm Alex. You?"

The boy caught on this time, "I'm Robbie. I thought mermaids had fins instead of legs!"

Alex just managed to stop her face from dropping into the palm of her hand at that assertion. It was her own fault — two attempts at jokes? She should have known better.

"She ain't a mermaid," the elder boy finally found his words, and Alex turned back to him with some relief. This time, his gaze actually met hers.

"Now we're getting somewhere — and eye contact too! Good job..." she ended with a nod meant to draw out the boy's name, and he actually took the hint.

"Sam," he said, frowning at the 'eye contact' bit.

Alex figured she best press on before he caught up: "So tell me if I'm wrong... your oars went over the side and you need to get home?"

She made that assessment quickly, based on the fact that she saw no oars.

"He dropped 'em over when we was trying to pull in a net!" Robbie declared from the bow. "Now we're going to be wrecked!"

Alex frowned at the dire forecast, "Obviously not — I'm here. But you could have been, so let this be a lesson... about oars..." It was actually even more awkward when she tried to be serious, so she stopped. "Forget it. Where's home?"

Robbie turned and pointed the way from which the boat had drifted. Alex had swum in from the opposite direction, so she supposed there had to be an outport fishing village somewhere ahead.

"Just over in the next cove," Sam added context.

That was all she needed to know: "Good. Home

time."

Glad to have a good reason to escape, Alex planted her feet on the bottom of the dory and then launched herself up into the air. The boys tried to follow with their eyes, but she moved too fast — all they could see was the small splash when she re-entered her beloved water.

She knew the boys were lucky: had they drifted too much further and been caught in a coastal current, or if the weather had turned and the sea gone heavy on them, they could have truly been lost. But as she surfaced at the stern of the boat and planted her hands on its narrow transom, she knew they'd be getting a deserved reprieve — and hopefully would learn a lesson too.

"Hold on," she warned as she started kicking her legs.

Sam leaned back over the stern with wide eyes, and fortunately he planted his hands on the sides at the same time — when the dory started motoring across the water he was just able to keep from falling over.

The boat was heavy, but hardly too much for Alex to move — Champion and all — so she got up a good turn of speed and guided it towards the next cove. As she went, she looked up to the right and watched as the cliff fell away behind her. It was soon replaced by similar rock faces, but as she turned into the next cove, she saw the headlands begin to slope away from the water, with bright green grass climbing all over them.

This was a beautiful place... so much of Alex's home island was lovely, and she figured she could spend a life-time swimming around it, or climbing over it, without managing to discover all its secrets.

The water was shoaling beneath her now, and though the wide hull of the dory eclipsed her view of the beach ahead, she was starting to hear sounds of commotion from shore. A boat that had gone out under the power of oars was coming back with a motor. That was causing a bit of a sensation.

As the rocky bottom gradually came up under Alex's feet, she switched from kicking to walking. That let her stand, and as the water grew shallower she was able to see over the boat. Sure enough, an outport lay ahead. Small houses, some on stilts to keep them level over uneven ground, were lined up along a narrow stretch of rocky beach, and the whole tiny population of the place was hurrying down to the water's edge, releasing some cries of surprise.

Then they all fell silent as they got a look at the lanky girl pushing the dory out of the water.

With a last few heaves, Alex moved the boat right up onto the beach, sliding it over the smooth pebbles before letting it settle. That done, she took a step back and planted her hands on her hips with a slightly heroic smile. The two boys hopped out without explaining what was going on; they simply joined the two-dozen gawkers who all stared at Alex, and after a moment of quiet the soon-to-be-named Lady Smith decided she should break the silence.

"Nothing to worry about," she lifted one hand casually and waved to her audience. "Robbie and Sam just needed some help getting back. I was floating by so I stopped to lend a hand."

Perhaps that sounded a little too gallant, but Alex figured this might be the right time to come across like a

Champion. At first the only answer she got was more silence; apparently the visual and the words didn't align so well. Then one of the oldest men from the village managed to respond, saying exactly what every one of his fellows was thinking: "*Wha*?"

Alex wasn't sure how to answer, but before she could even think to try, one of the women of the outport came forward in a hurry, "My God child, you'll catch your death of cold! Come inside and wrap up... glory be, you're starting to shiver... we better get you wrapped up or you'll be killed..."

As the woman approached, Alex held up her hands, "No it's quite alright, I've been swimming all day..."

"Were you shipwrecked? Oh my child..." another of the men from the outport seemed properly horrified.

Alex began to shake her head just as the woman produced a blanket and tried to wrap it around her: "No... no I swam up from Jimmystown..."

She tried to slip away from the blanket, but even her Champion speed wasn't quite sufficient to escape the mothering instincts of a Newfoundland missus, "You're skinny as anything, child! We better warm you up and get some food into you before you starve to death." The woman closed the blanket around Alex and then tried to start guiding her up the beach... only to find the girl wasn't so easy to budge as her slim form suggested. "Wha... come on, love..."

Alex shook her head, "No, you don't understand. I'm a Champion. You know, children of the savages of the new world... genetically changed by the Hubrin blue men so that I'm stronger and faster... from Lady Emily's Academy... you do know what I'm talking about?"

As her explanation drew blank looks from the people of the outport, Alex began to wonder exactly how far she'd actually swum that day. Probably a good idea to turn back before she was never heard from again.

"I'm very sorry, but I must leave you all. I'll try to visit again some day — lovely place you have here..." she deftly slipped the woman's grip, and her blanket, and was backing into the sea before anyone quite realized she'd made the move. The water was up to her waist when the onlookers fixed their gazes on her again... and then with a wave, she turned and dove into the North Atlantic.

She left stunned silence in her wake — stunned until Robbie ran to the water's edge and shouted, "Goodbye mermaid!"

That was about as logical an explanation for what he'd seen as he could figure, because he'd never bothered to learn about Champions. None of the people in this outport had much experience with them, and as they watched one swim off, they just had to shake their heads.

Returning to her husband's side, the woman who'd aimed to save Alex from freezing and starvation began folding up her rejected blanket, "She's some skinny."

Her husband nodded, but observed: "She has a pretty face, though."

With that his missus glared at him, then turned away from the beach, "Looked sour to me. And you'll be cooking your own supper tonight, Mister."

Despite being halfway out of the cove, Alex did catch that exchange (again, Champion hearing). She grimaced at the word choice but decided to ignore it. After all, Casanova gull hadn't thought her sour.

Though that probably wasn't a great vote of confidence.

There really was no way that train of thought could continue without being awkward, so Alex gave up and just swam for home. Her new life as a Champion awaited, and she was sure it would be much more dignified.

Probably.

Jennifer Combden

Jennifer Combden is a meteorologist living in St. John's, Newfoundland. She is a sponge for knowledge, and her love of learning is second only to her love of sharing that knowledge. Jennifer prefers to write science fiction, with a strong emphasis on the science, as a medium by which to explain complex ideas.

Combden's work will be recognized for her story 'Sulfer Bridges' *Flights from the Rock*.

In May 2018, Combden won the monthly Kit Sora Flash Fiction prize for her short story 'Tarnished,' which went on to be featured in the *Kit Sora: The Artobiography* collection.

Sunny Days

When asked what their favorite part of the solar system is, most people will reply with Earth, Jupiter, Mars, or another planet. Very few will answer with our sun. When asked about our sun, people often answer with friendly adjectives, describing the sun as a happy thing. While it is essential for our survival, the sun is not the calm, yellow ball in picture books. It is a boiling ball of plasma, a million times bigger than the Earth with a magnetic field that is twisting itself into knots until the whole field breaks down. As the magnetic field destroys itself every 11 years, it produces conditions ripe for sunspots and flares. When this magnetic energy builds up, occasionally the sun will eject part of itself during a flare. This solar material can move at speeds up to 1.5 million km/h, with as much energy as a billion-megaton nuclear bomb.

Thankfully Earth is not defenseless. We have our own magnetic field, which deflects most of the ejected matter away from us, keeping both our atmosphere and us safe. While the field is getting pummeled, we earthlings get to enjoy the auroras that result from the buildup of energy.

"Does anyone have any questions for Dr. Elizabeth

Williams about the sun?" Mrs. Sharon asked her grade seven students, most of who hadn't even noticed that the presentation was over. After a short pause, she turned to me and shook my hand. "Thank you so much for coming, Doctor, it's always a treat to have a real scientist come to our class."

While the class was applauding, I gathered my presentation, thanked them for listening, and quietly made my exit. I'm a researcher at the Goddard Space Center, and when kids see that NASA logo on your presentation, they tend to get excited until they realize you aren't an astronaut. I mulled this over in my mind while I walked back to the center, eager to get back to my work.

"Miss me?" I called out to my partner in crime and fellow researcher, Gary Hawthorn.

"It's been pretty quiet here. Nothing interesting across the board," he replied without looking up. Glancing at his screen, I saw he was watching one of the current active regions of the sun, which featured a number of strong sunspots, and what looked like the beginning of a solar prominence.

"How long has that been there?" I said, pointing to the small arch of solar material.

"Hmm, not long?" Gary switched to the archive images we stored and flipped through the most recent ones. "Looks like it's only been there a couple of hours. Might be a good one yet!"

I reached over to his keyboard and brought up the image of the sun again, looking it over. Spots and prominences were nice for some of the researchers here, but our work didn't start until those arches broke and came sailing our way. However, you couldn't tell by looking if a prominence might turn into a flare until right before it happened. Even our best equipment only gave us a little extra warning, which was why most of our instruments were constantly recording.

I swatted Gary and said, "Come on, we have a status report to give." I grabbed my files as I spoke. The head of our department liked to have updates every week or two, so that when her boss wanted a report of our progress, she'd have more than a vague idea of what we were doing.

The difference between administrator offices and researcher offices never ceased to amaze me. Our office was the definition of organized chaos. We knew where everything was, but God help us if someone else had to find something. Dr. Amy Driedzic's office on the other hand looked like it came out of a catalog, and screamed, 'I'm an important administrator'. Luckily Dr. Driedzic herself was more down to earth, and these regular status reports weren't too much of a chore. While she didn't start off as a sun researcher herself, she was a PhD in astrophysics and knew what we were talking about.

We all shook hands and I handed her a copy of our latest briefing. We sat down, and after the required pleasantries I started to explain why we were here giving another report only one day after our last report.

"As you know, we're in another solar maximum, the time during the solar cycle when sunspots are most numerous, so all this increased activity is to be expected. However, over the last few days we've noticed a dramatic increase in the number of prominences being formed in the high activity areas. An unpredicted increase." At the word 'unpredicted,' Dr. Driedzic's eyebrows shot up. We might not know much concerning the whys of the sun, but we had its cycles fairly well mapped.

I went through all the numbers, with Gary jumping in on occasion to provide additional theories. Evidently all this intrigued Dr. Driedzic, as she canceled her next appointment so we could keep going over information with her. We were close to cluing up when I felt my beeper vibrating, and at the same time Gary grabbed his pocket - his was going off as well. The only thing we used them for was to keep tabs on what data was coming into the lab, and only if something major was going on.

Explaining this to Dr. Driedzic, we all took off towards our lab. Passing other offices, we could see that the whole wing was frantic. Something major was happening.

Without even sitting down, Gary tapped out a keycode on his computer, causing a data dump to the printer. I went to my station and called up the live graphs that our beepers were tied to.

"What the hell is going on here?" Dr. Driedzic cried out, her voice showing signs of stress. While we were busy trying to dig through the data, more alarms had started going off, including a flashing light Gary had added as a joke a few years earlier.

"If we knew, we'd tell you. None of this data makes sense; it shouldn't be possible," I replied, trying to translate the peaked graphs in front of me into something explainable. We hadn't made our scales big enough to deal with the incoming data.

"I have the raw data here; I don't have time to plot it,

but based on just the light and x-ray output, and the speed this thing is moving, we have something big happening," Gary said.

I called up the archival photos for the last hour and scanned through them quickly. The little arch of sun I was looking at earlier had grown into a large prominence in a much shorter time than the usual few weeks. Grabbing my own copy of the raw data, I started trying to piece it all together in my head.

"From the looks of it, we had a sharp twist in the sun's magnetic field, which caused the prominence to form a flare much faster than it normally would. All that extra energy is making this thing a lot bigger than your average ejection. Gary, do you have the speed figured out yet?" I was trying to keep Dr. Driedzic in the loop, but we had to get to the bottom of this and fast.

"Just about, should be printing off now."

We both dashed to the printer, with Dr. Driedzic crowding in as well. The paper almost tore as both Gary and I grabbed for it at the same time.

"Well?" Dr. Driedzic said impatiently, clearly not impressed with the way we kept ignoring her. But we were scientists, not administrators. I wasn't about to say something unless I was sure of what I was saying. Gary and I quickly went over what all this data could mean in quiet whispers. Finally, I stood up straight and faced Dr. Driedzic.

"We're in deep shit."

"Well, that's all well and good. Too bad there isn't a scientist here to explain to me exactly what that means," Dr. Driedzic quipped.

"What she means," Gary said stepping in front of me, "is that we have an extremely high energy blast of particles headed towards us at speeds in excess of 10 million kilometers per hour. This is the biggest one on record, and it's headed straight for us."

It quickly became apparent why Dr. Driedzic had such a high administrator position. Before Gary had even finished his sentence, she was on the phone, making terse conversation with a number of other people. Not even five minutes had passed before she turned to us and said, "You have an hour to get a presentation together to explain to those with at-risk properties what is about to happen."

"You know I hate doing presentations, you're the speaker for the group." Gary complained. I wasn't going to admit it, but I wasn't looking forward to giving this presentation either.

"Just pretend you're doing another elementary school one, these guys probably know as much about our work as those kids," I said in my most calming voice, trying to convince him as much as myself.

"Yeah, kids with multi-million dollar equipment which is about to be destroyed," he muttered, as much to himself as to me.

"You guys are up. Try not to scare them too much?" I looked at the young women beckoning us onto the stage, steeled myself, and stepped out, dragging Gary behind me.

"At 9:24 this morning, the sun started showing signs of unusual activity. This was not entirely unexpected as we are in a solar maximum, a time of increased solar activity. However, in a matter of hours, what started as a routine phenomenon escalated into an event of magnitude we have never seen in recorded history.

"In laymen's terms, the sun has produced a rapid solar flare pointed directly at earth. The initial radiation has already come and gone; what's left to hit are the highly-energetic ionized particles that have been ejected from the sun.

"Flares occur frequently, especially during a solar maximum, and normally we would never notice it. This is because earth is protected by a magnetic field that deflects most of these ionized particles away from our atmosphere. However the field isn't solid, and given enough bombardment, it can be overcome. We expect this to happen when this storm hits us.

"When it does hit, the first thing that will happen is the atmosphere will heat up and expand due to friction. This will produce extra drag on the satellites in orbit, causing many of them to fall to earth. The lower their orbit, the higher the chance is that they will succumb to the drag factor.

"The next, and possibly most damaging thing to happen is that the atmosphere will experience a build up of electric charge. As this charge seeks ground, it will travel along anything it can, pipelines and wires being the main targets. When this charge reaches transformers, it will cause catastrophic failures unless it is preempted.

"Engineers have already been dispatched to start a planned shut down of the entire North American grid. By disconnecting production plants from the grid they can be kept safe, however other equipment remains vulnerable. Only time will tell how much will actually be damaged.

"I can take a small number of questions now."

I stepped back and took a deep breath. I felt like I was back in Junior High speaking in front of the class, but I knew that I'd probably end up giving this speech a few times in the next couple of hours.

"You said this radiation has already hit the Earth, should we be worried? How big of a dose are we talking about?"

Gary stepped forward to take the question. We had agreed to trade off since we both had about the same level of knowledge on this topic. "It is a slightly higher level of radiation than we normally receive every day, but no worse than a few minutes in a tanning booth. The problem really lies in electronic equipment that doesn't have enough shielding to deal with it, such as satellites outside of the protective ozone layer. The radiation can cause small programming errors that can lead to major malfunctions."

"How long do we have before this hits?"

I stepped to the microphone, checking my cheat notes for the exact times. "We estimate that the particles are moving at speeds in excess of six and a half million miles per hour. As of right now, our best estimate would be nine hours."

This caused quite a bit of an uproar in the room, with people making frantic calls and the press furiously typing up reports.

Dr. Cannon, the director of the Goddard Space Center, tried his best to quiet everyone. A press member stood and shouted, "What military presence can we expect during the black out?" while another yelled, "What are the damage estimates?"

"If anyone has any scientific questions, feel free to ask them now. All other questions will have to wait until the press conference in an hour. This is for information only; we are not in charge of making plans," Dr. Cannon said diplomatically, but still as if he was addressing a naughty two year-old. When no one replied, he said, "We have media and information packages for distribution, and a list of precautions to be distributed to the public. Any more questions of a scientific nature can be directed to our media relations office."

Following Dr. Cannon as he marched off stage, I felt a growing knot in my stomach. Studying solar storms and making extreme models was all right when they're theoretical, but when they actually start happening and you have to break the news, it's a whole different story.

Looking at Gary and I, Dr. Cannon's steeled look melted into one of worry. "What do we do now?"

"Not a damn thing," I said, sliding into a chair. "It's already happened. It's up to the engineers now, not the theoretical scientists."

Letting out a small "Humf," Dr. Cannon stalked off towards his office.

"We should probably back everything up," Gary said after Dr. Cannon had disappeared around a corner. "The servers are liable to take a beating."

I nodded, glad for some busy work. "We should gather what emergency supplies we have too. Give me your keys, I'll go by both our places, get what I can, and bring it back here."

Gary tossed me his house keys. "Let the others in the wing know to do it too; between all of us we're likely to cover all the bases."

I went through the wing, which mostly housed other scientists in our field, telling everyone to back up their data to some non-magnetic format, and gather some supplies if they were planning to stay here. Most agreed with me that we were better off in larger numbers, and a few even decided to bring their families here rather than stay at home. They had all seen the data when it came in, so luckily I didn't have to go into long explanations of why we needed so much prep for a planned blackout.

With both Gary and I being unattached researchers, I figured he'd have as much in the way of canned food as me. After letting myself into his place, I was not disappointed, finding plenty of food that would keep well. I also took a bunch of stuff from his freezer, knowing that we should be able to keep it cold back at the lab. I knew Gary was an avid camper too, so I scouted around for that gear. Tucked away in a closet, he had a couple of sleeping bags and foam pads, a gas stove, and a few other useful items. I also grabbed all the batteries, flashlights, and candles I found during my quick search.

I locked his place up as tight as I could, including putting all the curtains down, and made my way to my place. Passing a gas station on the way, I could see that people had already started lining up. I had been thinking of stopping in somewhere to buy some supplies, but decided against trying to fight the crowds. I didn't want to even think about how insane people would start getting between now and the blackout, let alone what would happen *after* the blackout.

I arrived at my house in twice the time it would normally take me to make the trip thanks to the traffic, but I wasn't very rushed. I hadn't heard any official reports, but I knew that it would take a few hours at least for the engineers to plan, let alone execute, the shut down sequence. We had only warned them an hour before the conference. Really, they'd be lucky if they managed to do it before the material hit, but that wasn't going to stop people from thinking it was going to happen in the next thirty seconds.

Because I knew where everything was in my house, loading the car took a lot less time than at Gary's. I didn't have a lot of equipment to offer, but I did have a few battery-free gizmos that people keep giving me for Christmas. I packed some clothes, cursing that I didn't think of doing that at Gary's, and all my sheets, blankets, and towels. Deciding I should go back for some more of Gary's stuff, I locked my place and headed back to do that.

I arrived back at our office about two hours later. Gary had apparently been busy, with stacks of DVDs and printouts around him.

"Much more to go?" I asked, causing him to jump and knock over a stack of paper. "Good thing you used the old feeder paper rather than the loose stuff," I laughed.

"That would be precisely why I used the connected paper," Gary said, apparently in good spirits. "Need some help unloading?"

"Yes, please."

Gary stuck another blank DVD in the drive and set that burning and got up again. "Dave next door has taken over the emergency preparations. He's figured out how to store and distribute everything."

"Figures - he's a Boy Scout or something isn't he?" I asked as I went out the door.

"Scout Master is the proper term for adults," Dave answered for himself, nearly scaring me out of my wits. He was wearing a large grin.

"You seem to be enjoying yourself," I said, raising an eyebrow.

"Well, y'know, gotta keep your spirits up to stay productive. Why not enjoy it if you can?"

I nodded, deciding that he probably was the best guy to have in charge. It took a couple of trips for Gary and I to get everything back into the complex. Dave informed us that all electronics (including my battery less radio) needed to be stored in one of the x-ray rooms.

The x-ray rooms were lead lined rooms that also had a grounded wire grid in the walls. They were fairly large since they also doubled as bomb and storm shelters. We carted a load of stuff there, and left it with the person who seemed to be in charge of keeping an inventory on all of it. It seemed a little strange to see so many paper lists being used, but really that was the only way to be sure it wouldn't get wiped. I noticed a number of hard drives stored there as well and I asked about it.

"Well, we aren't sure how much room we'll have for everything, so we told people we would only be storing a couple of full computers for reading the drives. No sense wasting space when all you really need is a few, right?" the young man answered, while processing our load.

"This place is being run like an army camp; I wasn't gone that long!" I commented to Gary in awe on our way back to our wing.

"Well, everything was a little chaotic when people first started bringing stuff in, but Dave really stepped up and started giving everyone something to do. He's even got a mini daycare set up so that their parents can get everything ready. Some of the relatives think we're over-preparing, but better safe than sorry. We'll be here for a few days at best anyway, and as Dave mentioned, the general public is great at reacting poorly during an inevitable crisis and there is safety in numbers. That argument won most of them over."

Gary was about to say something else when someone grabbed our arms. "Come on, we need help moving more stuff."

On our third trip back in from someone's truck, I spotted a cross-looking Dr. Amy Driedzic. She seemed to be on a warpath with her target being Dave. I was a fair distance away from the pair, but could already hear her.

"What the hell do you think you're doing, Dr. Young? I know you got my message; I closed the building an hour ago. What are all these people doing here? It looks like you're loading the damn ark! What's this I hear about you using the server room as a refrigerator? You people need to go home!"

Drawing himself up to his full 6' 4" height, Dave looked the picture of a drill sergeant. "Yeah, we all know we don't have to be here. You've closed the building before and we've still come in and you didn't take issue then. All these people either work here or are related to people who work here, and so are allowed in the building. The server room is designed to keep its temperature low even if the main cooling system fails, and the x-ray rooms are perfect to keep the vital electronics safe. So if you have a problem with these plans, feel free to tell all these folks that they need to pack everything up and go home."

Crossing his arms, he waited for her to respond. Surveying the area, Dr. Driedzic sighed, knowing she wasn't going to win the argument. "I'm not about to kick you out of here, but the doors will be locked in about an hour and I don't want people propping them open!"

Dave gave Dr. Driedzic a three-fingered salute, beaming. Dr. Driedzic rolled her eyes and marched back in the direction of her own office. As soon as she was out of sight, he started giving orders again, and everyone went back to work getting ready.

Back in our office, Gary and I decided that we needed to clear the place out if we were going to be staying there for a few days, especially since we were liable to have guests in it. There were an abundance of empty banker boxes going around, so we got to work filing away all the back ups and throwing out anything that wasn't needed.

"Have you listened to any of the news reports?" I asked Gary while chasing stray pop cans out from under my desk.

"Yeah, why?"

"When's the power supposed to go out?"

"About an hour before the storm hits, they're estimating. They're going to be cutting it pretty fine."

I checked my watch. "So we have about 3 hours?"

"Guess so. I think they're going to start distributing candles and such soon. Which means we need to speed up if we're going to keep this place from being a death trap. Loose paper and open flames aren't happy roommates. "

Despite the filing, there was still a lot of junk around. Labeling a dozen or more boxes, we moved them out to one of the storage rooms. We kept all our back up data in the office, even though it was just as safe in the storage room. It was bad enough knowing we were likely going to lose a lot of equipment; we couldn't stand to risk losing what data we had too. Dismantling our computers, we pulled out the hard drives to store as well, and put the towers out of the way. By the time an intern came around with a box of supplies for us, the office had been gutted and made livable. One advantage to having worked here for years was that our office was actually quite large. Of course, you couldn't really tell when there were piles of papers and equipment everywhere, but once cleaned up it was a good spot.

We went about setting up air mattresses, organizing our personal belongings, and putting a flashlight within easy reach of the door. By the time everything was set up, the office looked more like a camp bunk than a research station.

With nothing left to do, we wandered out in what had become the common area where most of the others had already gathered around a TV showing CNN. After watching it intently for a few minutes, I discovered that my theory was right, and that there was just the usual repeating of a few facts, with a whole lot of panic thrown in. The only useful bit of information conveyed was that the power companies were in the final stages of shutting down the grid.

For such a large group, we were all very calm. I tried to imagine what some other groups might be doing, with visions of crying children and panicking adults. Deciding that the picture was too depressing, I tried to focus on the happy kids who were running around the edges of our gathering. A few adults were playing cards, laughing, and looking very calm. I'm sure every one of them had the same knot in their stomach as me, but we had plans, and others to lean on, so we knew we'd be okay.

I tried to act as calm as the others, but I was chewing my nails down to the quick. I signed up to be a theoretical scientist because I hated having to deal with practical matters. I hated having practical matters forced upon me even more, but here we were. As I watched Gary argue with the top scientist on CNN over the sun facts they were giving out, I wondered how much longer I'd have to wait before things would start to get interesting.

And then the world went black.

Immune

Mommy said, don't worry, it's just a cold. I don't like colds, but Mommy's always right. She was sick first, then Daddy. A few days later, Mike was sick too. It takes longer for kids to show *symptoms*, Daddy said. I don't think he knew I was listening, but I was. I'm always listening.

I knew before Daddy that Mommy wasn't breathing anymore. I hid under the bed so I could listen when Daddy found her, so cold and stiff. I heard him crying about how it was all his fault, and Mike screaming about how he killed us all, made us all sick. I wanted to tell him that we weren't all sick, that I was ok. I wanted to make Daddy feel better, but I had to stay quiet.

Mike got sicker, and didn't get up much anymore. Daddy slept a lot so I watched TV. The news people kept talking about *pandemics* and that police were looking for where it all started. They mentioned where Daddy worked, but I didn't know what it meant. I hate not knowing what things mean.

Daddy got mad when I asked him about where he worked. I asked Mike when he got up to eat, and he said Daddy made the bug that made us all sick. That it was only supposed to be for the bad guys, but it got out. Like a monster in the closet that doesn't stay there.

Daddy doesn't move anymore. Mike said we should put him in the cold room, but he sleeps too much to do it. I just keep the door closed. I try to keep feeding Mike cereal, but he doesn't wake up much either. There are new people on the TV, they say don't worry.

Staying up late isn't that fun with no one around. I'm not allowed to use the stove, but I'm tired of cereal. I got some soup warm without burning myself. I tried to get Mike to eat some, but he doesn't wake up anymore. He's really warm all the time, but Mommy keeps the fever stuff locked.

Mike's door stays closed now. The house really smells, but I don't know what else to do. Everything is so quiet; there are no cars going by or anything. I spend most of the time watching movies. I tried one of Daddy's hidden movies, but it was really boring.

I was drawing when I heard something outside, first time in days. I could see a big van slowing coming up the driveway, with a satellite on top of it. They go to the neighbor's first, then start coming here. I want to hide, but I'm so tired of being alone. I like listening, but the TV doesn't say anything. I open the door for the men who are wearing yellow suits with tents on their heads. I can't understand what they say, but one, who was actually a lady, tells me to come with them.

It's quiet here too, but at least the doctors talk to me. They had to put me in isolation because of the bug Daddy made. They keep telling me not to be mad at Daddy; that he didn't mean to hurt anyone. They tell me that I'm the cure! I don't like all the needles and stuff, but I got to have McDonald's which was better than soup and cereal.

Report ID: 363974-c
Filed by: CLASSIFIED
Retrieved: CLASSIFIED

Despite her above-average intelligence, the patient does not seem to realize how she came to survive this plague. We hope that she continues to consider herself lucky, immune by chance. However, based on her family profile, curiosity will likely become evident. It is the recommendation of this council that she remain under surveillance indefinitely.

PERSONAL COMMUNIQUE
DESTROY IMMEDIATELY

You have no idea WHY he would inoculate his daughter but no one else in his family? We know he's been working on genetic tampering, do you think those army types have caught on? Keep all information to yourself; don't need them trying to dissect the poor girl. Any luck on cracking his files? Best Wishes, Kate.

Matthew LeDrew

Matthew LeDrew holds an Honours Degree in English from the Memorial University of Newfoundland with a minor in Anthropology, and studied Journalism at College of the North Atlantic in Stephenville, Newfoundland. He was honoured to be a jury member of both the 2018 NLBA awards and the 2020 Arts and Letters Awards.

He has written twenty-one novels for Engen Books: the ten book Coral Beach Casefiles series, *The Long Road, Cinders, Sinister Intent, Faith, Family Values, Fate's Shadow, Jacobi Street, Touch Your Nose, Infinity, The Tourniquet Reprisal*, and *Exodus of Angels* the latter three of which with co-author Ellen Curtis.

He lives in St. John's, Newfoundland.

The Shoe

To the untrained eye…

"Look here, sir!" Daniel shouted, his arms waving frantically. He dropped the small pick and brush that he had been using to dig in the delicate soil, turning to stare at his supervisor, Thomas Hopkins. Hopkins was busy flirting with one of the younger tour-guides, as usual, and looked very upset that Thomas had interrupted him. Maybe he wouldn't have been so mad if this hadn't been the fourth time that he had been interrupted. "Sir!" he shouted again as he clamoured around tremendous boulders and slipped on loose pebbles, finally stopping in front of his superior and bending over, his hands on his knees, trying to catch his breath as the sweat dripped from his forehead, moistening the desert-like sand that blew around them constantly, getting in their eyes and making the dig unbearable. "I really think I've found something this time, sir!"

Hopkins rolled his eyes and sighed heavily, not wanting to tear himself away from the sixteen-year-old blonde long enough to let Daniel discover move oddly shaped rocks and quartz. "Winters, I swear to Gawd. If this is another stupid dog bone, I will implant my foot so far into your- "

"No!" Daniel insisted, motioning over and again with his hands to come and see, the excitement emanating from each and every one of his pours, creating a stench that was not quite welcoming. "It's real this time! I swear! It's not even like a rock."

Hopkins frowned. "It's not solid? What the hell is it then?"

"I don't know... I think I've discovered some new artefact of the Now Yak Clan!"

A spark lit up in Thomas Hopkins' eyes, a sly smile spreading across his lips. He rubbed his chin, thinking of all the money that a brand new find would bring to the dig. *How many more slutty young tour girls could I get with an extra mill?* he thought whimsically, then discarded the thought and followed Daniel down the rickety old step ladder to where he'd unbrushed his little discovery.

Hopkins squinted against the harsh desert sun as Winters pulled out the centuries old artifact, holding it up for his eyes to see. His eyes went wide as they adjusted to the light, and he took in what had been displayed before him, his mouth watering as though it were one of his wife's four course meals. "My God," he whispered softly, his fingers trembling as he carefully took it from his trainee.

It was about a foot in length, but only a few inches wide. It was dingy and dirty with wear and dust, but still held some amount of sheen to its black surface. The bottom of it was hard, and oddly patterned with spirals and stars, and lines intersecting one another over and over again. However, that hard part gave way a half-inch up the item, giving way to a different material. While still black, there were spots of grey, and a weird checkmark of the side of it was the only color therein, bright and vibrant red. It still retained some smell, like the hide of a cow once it had been dried for several days in the warm summer sun. This part appeared hard like the first, but when Hopkins touched it, it gave way slightly beneath his finger. He pulled back suddenly, afraid of damaging it, then tried again with more care. It was smooth save for the tiny lines drawn in it, apparently for decoration. At the very peak was a hole that proved it was hollow, followed by a flimsy strap and several intertwining strands of felt, not terribly unlike string.

"Is that string?" Daniel asked, as if reading his mind.

"Don't be absurd!" Thomas chuckled, ruffling the boy's hair. "The Now Yak's were nowhere near pre-industrial. They couldn't have mass-produced string like we do!"

Daniel frowned, dismayed at his own stupidity. It faded after a moment, replaced again by the genuine wonder that was before him. The discovery of a lifetime. "What do you suppose it was used for?"

After a moment's thought, Hopkins smiled. He placed the hole over his right hand so that the star patterns faced upwards, tightening it with the straps and letting the flap rest against his palm for support. "Obviously, it is used in conjunction with a compass. You see, you would line this red marker up with true north, and then lift off in your space-craft and follow this map to the stars."

"You believe that the Now Yak's were capable of space travel?"

"No... Certainly not. More likely, it was left here as a learning tool for them by visitors of a long-extinct alien race."

Daniel hummed in acknowledgment, in awe of his teacher's seemingly infinite wisdom. "What is it called, Sir?"

Hopkins examined the item next to the red check mark, then smiled. "It is a shoe. Pronounced 'show'."

"A shoe. Amazing."

Invasion

Maria stood by the window, the teacup in her hand making long wreaths of steam that curled around her slender form. She was wearing the navy slacks I'd bought her two birthdays ago and had never seen her in and a simple gray top. Her arms were bare and she looked cold.

Far in the distance, not far from where Marlborough Mall would be, there was a tiny sliver of silver hovering in the air amidst a sea of perfect blue. It caught the light, but did not reflect it. It almost looked as though it had been painted onto the outside of the window, like a dime-store decal meant to amuse the young and the stupid.

Maria stared at it intently, and I saw a shiver run through her.

I tried to say something to her, then stopped and looked down at my tea. I watched as the steam from it turned my glasses into a world of fog, and then slowly ebb back to normal until it just hung near the corners of my vision.

"What do you think happened with Carol and David's kid after?" she asked finally, her eyes still fixed on the dull line on the horizon.

I paused and looked at her. Her breasts were pressing against the cotton of her shirt. I cleared my throat, realizing that I had been unintentionally staring at them for some time.

"I'm not sure," I said finally, picking up my cup with both hands and holding it in front of my face. The heat from the tea cascaded against my chin and neck, making them so hot that I could feel tiny beads of sweat form on them immediately. "It was a pretty bad thing what he did, breaking into the school like that. He tore the hell out of that old grand piano."

"Yeah," she said, and for a moment I thought I'd lost her yet again to the world outside our window. "I don't think that was him though, I think it was that other boy -- Johnny. I can't imagine Tyson getting something like that into his head all on his own."

"On Good Friday no less," I huffed.

She turned away from the window and rolled her eyes at me. "I don't think anyone but you and Missus Engleman realized it was Good Friday."

She sat down across from me at the table and laid her tea down in front of her. After a moment, she picked up the milk tin and added a healthy splash to her already pale drink, then stirred it absently with the sugar spoon.

I watched her, the way she sunk into the dusky walls behind her and became two-dimensional. I felt tears well up behind my eyes and turn everything into a murky gray mush, and then forced them back with a long sniff.

I felt stupid.

"I finally found something for your Dad for his birthday," she said. "It's a book with all these different types of birds in it. The pictures are drawn by that painter he loves, Nathan Shaw?"

"*Nigel* Shaw."

"Nigel Shaw."

Her palms clasped around her mug for warmth. There was none to be found anymore, the steam was gone and the tea inside was cold and filmy. She bit her lip. "What do you think they want?"

I frowned deeply and sadly, then got up and wrapped my arms around her as tightly as I dared.

Outside the saucer still spun, hovering over Marlborough with its dull gray sheen.

The Chair

The memories of my childhood are viewed through a deep fog not easily penetrated.

I grew up in a small town near the easternmost tip of Newfoundland, in a place known for deep mists and heavy rain that hit with maniacal, unfettered fury.

The landscape consisted of many rises and valleys; the upside of this was that bike riding became a smooth and swift experience. The downside was the cliffs.

Jagged maws of stone bent this way and that, stretching far into the water in some places and retraced deep into bowel-like caves in others. Some went high, leaning forward over the cape below like oppressive overlords, others simply rose and fell in smooth, uneventful lumps.

To a ten year old, even the most hazardous of these were not obstacles, but challenges.

I haven't been back to this place in nearly ten years, and am amazed by the difference time has made. Erosion has made rock faces that used to seem scalable - - *were* scalable, I remember intently - - now seem insurmountable.

There was once a large head of rock that hung out

over a narrow cave, providing shelter enough for camp-fires and barbeques consisting chiefly of Vienna sausages and Cola. I recall discovering a delightful trick: that if you placed an unopened can of sausages in the fire and left them there, the pressure would blow the lid off and leave the contents perfectly cooked. Let the others roast their wienies on sticks if they pleased... I was a much smarter caveman.

That rock face is gone now, leaving a sheer cliff. If not for the scorched circle of rocks where many fires had been before, I might not have recognized it.

I pick up one of the blackened stones and jerk back, feeling heat when my flesh first touches the smooth shale. When I grab it again, it's as cold as the rest of the beach, wet from the lapping kisses of the sea. I hold it, its weight changing my impression of it somehow, making it tactile and real. I bounce it in my palm several times, then turn and whip it into the waves.

It disappears long before it hits the water, into a soupy fog I hadn't even realized was rolling in, stretching and swirling and trying to get to shore.

Around the side of the cliff, just to the left of the fire-place, the beach stops and gives way to a grassy knoll. It's a lush green even now, fighting the chill of fall as long as it can. It rises slowly to connect three of the varying cliffs of the beach in peculiar ways, with foot trails worn from years of use linking them all, and it even led out to the main road beyond it, becoming a field that met with one of the aforementioned hills that dotted the small town. I recall being mocked by my childhood friends, Rick and Allan, for taking this route to the top on our races up the sheer cliff. Such things are inconceivable to me now... to climb these cliffs was dangerous enough, but to actually race up them seemed suicidal.

Standing near the base of the path, I remember the years spent here, running from one cliff to another. I had my first kiss with sea-foam caressing the bottom of my feet, sitting on the furthest point out on the rocks. I can't remember her name anymore, but I always remember how sweet her lips had tasted after sipping on a can of Cherry Cola.

I also remember the Chair.

Just to the edge of the grassy knoll, carved into the solid face of the cliff, was a Chair. It took imagination to see, of course, like the shapes found in clouds or the faces found hidden in the trunks of evergreen trees, but once seen it could not be unseen.

There was a legend that someone sat there, invisible except in the moments before death. He waited for children who fell while trying to overcome the cliff and opened up the earth to swallow them.

In the legend, it was called the Devil's Chair.

I remember daring to climb that side, once. Allan was already at the top of the adjacent cliff, and Rick and I were scaling the Chair. Rick was ahead of me and almost near the top, grunting as he overcame the peak.

When I reached it, I slipped on the mossy rock, yelping as I grabbed at the short green grass of the field above. I remember the way my feet felt dangling freely in the air, gravity seeming to tug at them with its weighty fingers. I also remember feeling heat tickle the soles of my shoes, although it was evening in late November.

My hands squeezed the ground so tight that green juice pushed itself out of the grass, clods of dirt squishing between my fingers like kneads of dough.

Rick reached out and grabbed my arms by the wrist and pulled with everything he had, his teeth clenching and his blonde hair falling in front of his face.

"Come on!" he yelled, angry and concerned all at once.

As my feet kicked freely and Rick pulled me up, I turned over my shoulder and saw it. Saw Him.

He was sitting on the edge of his seat, shimmering black talons gripping at the arms of his chair in anticipation. His head was craned upward to see me, straining his neck to the breaking point, and he wore a smile that literally escaped the sides of his face to reveal an impossible amount of teeth. They were yellow, and stank of sulphur.

Rick pulled me up and I heard the creature howl. It reached up with those claws, each one at least as thick as my leg, and scraped for me; trying with its last futile effort to bat me from my friend's grasp and finding only dirt.

Rick and I never spoke of the event, and not long after we both went off to high school and drifted apart.

He'd gone into construction and moved into the city, made a good living for himself. He'd fallen from the scaffolding of a high-rise he'd been working on and landed on his back some nine stories down. For some reason, it made me remember that evening, years ago, when he'd saved me from a similar fate, and I got in my car and just drove until I'd found myself here.

I walk along the trail to the top of the cliff, all the while hearing Allan mocking me for doing so. When I reach the top, I can see over the fog and watch it stretch out for miles along the top of the water.

Smiling, I look down at the grassy patch where Rick and I had lay, chuckling and gasping with exasperation and adrenaline.

My mouth goes dry and my feet go numb, so much so that I almost lose my balance.

There are five long gouges in the grass, burned into brown streaks where life has refused to grow, leading to the edge of the cliff.

I swallow, and feel the heat against my back.

Samuel Bauer

Samuel Bauer is a proud mathematician, Shad alumni, and part-time storyteller.

Sam is one of only a handful of authors to be featured in over three From the Rock volumes. His stories include 'The Locket,' 'Precious Pieces Unknown,' 'Dark Peaks,' 'Nucklavee,' and 'In the Rising Flame.'

The Locket

An excerpt from the files of St. Dymphna Hospital for the Mentally Ill (1845-1896), published for the interest of the public.

Found written on the back of R. Cole's patient file sheet:

What I have to say concerning the late Mr. Theodore Loft is unusual in the extreme, and as such, has no suitable space on our standard forms. Mr. Loft arrived to us from the nearby HMQ Mental Hospital, owing to the fact that the psychiatric ward there was overflowing, and Mr. Loft had no known next of kin or associates.

As noted on the patient file sheet, Mr. Loft suffered from hallucinations. These hallucinations were distressing in the extreme, and resulted in regular, but not frequent, violent and self-damaging outbursts. He would attempt to end the hallucinations by damaging his eyes or ears, and attack anybody nearby who attempted to stop him. Preceding these episodes, he would mumble incoherently about a "Matilda", apologizing and acting as if she was conversing with him. He would ignore any stimuli, other than to resist the nurses attempting to restrain him from self-harm. After a short period of about thirty seconds, he would then attempt to gouge out his own eyes, or become extremely violent towards the nurses. Immediately upon recovering, he would fall into a fitful sleep.

In the three months that he was here, he had twelve outbursts, and severely injured two nurses, Mrs. Holloway and my wife, Joan. Mrs. Holloway has since recovered and now is working with more peaceful patents. Upon discovering that he had injured Mrs. Holloway, Mr. Loft came to my office and asked if he was still allowed to stay, as he had grown to love the south gardens that he tended. I told him of course he was allowed to stay, and he could stay until he was ready to leave. One month later, he injured Joan. This time, I was the one who was there when he woke up. He was mortified, and I reassured him that he could stay. The next outburst, his heart was put under so much pressure that he died.

I had conversed with the man, in hopes of finding out what tortured him. He was reluctant to tell me what it was exactly, but he told me of how he was a simple farmhand, living in barns and working for food and lodgings. Whenever he was asked if he had a lover, he would fall silent and taciturn, and he would refuse any and all advances. He had few possessions when he came to the hospital, but his most prized was a locket around his neck. He never removed it except for sleeping and bathing, but even then he would not let it out of his sight. I never saw him look into it, but he was protective of it, and would not let anyone touch it.

After his death, I went through his possessions and found a will. It stated that he donated all of his possessions to the hospital, but that the locket must be buried with him. I looked through his possessions, and upon finding the small locket, I peered inside. I now wish that I had not.

As I opened it, I experienced a vision that filled my senses. The stench of burnt flesh tore at my nostrils, and I saw my wife Joan burning alive in a flame. Her pained screams tore at my ears. When I came to, I was in a cold sweat on the floor. The locket lay before me, opened. Engraved inside was D.F. I closed the foul thing, and buried it with the man. The terrible vision I hoped was buried with him. But some things cannot be sealed by mere earth.

Two months later, Joan and I moved to a small cottage just off of the grounds. My disposition had grown more nervous, and she felt that being away from the patients might alleviate my stress. On the third day, I returned home to my wife from the hospital, as she had taken ill recently and was nauseas, and as such, was staying at home resting. As I approached my house, a smell of smoke filled the air. My mouth grew dry as I recalled that terrible vision. As I began to run, the house became engulfed in flames.

The first thing I heard was the screams. Horror engulfed my mind, charring away any rational thought. I rushed inside and found my wife in the kitchen, passed out. I ran from the house. I laid her gently on the ground. I used my bare hands to put out the flames that covered her dress. I felt her wrist. There was no pulse. Desperate, I did what one should use to save a person who has drowned. I breathed into her nostril, and then applied pressure to her chest. I continued to simulate natural breathing, but all was in vain. She had perished.

I now write these words with scarred hands. The flames that stole my wife burned my body as well as my heart. When I walk these halls, often I hear her voice echoing back at me, unintelligibly. I hear the screams of newborns, though our hospital has no place for children. And sometimes, I can see her face, burnt and red, staring at me, with pleading eyes. And now, in the dead of night as I write these words, I can hear her footsteps coming nearer. She is calling out to me. Pleading as to why I could not save her. And my mouth is numb. I cannot speak, only mumble. Mumble out the words:

Joan, I'm sorry.

Dr. Rufus Cole, PHD.

Tara Murphy

Tara Murphy is a former archaeologist and graphic designer, and current makeup artist and carpenter. When she is not building houses, she can be found working in film and television. She spends more time planning than doing, and as a result, her to-do list is insurmountable. Future plans include making a Wookiee costume, assembling stormtrooper armour, and writing down more story ideas. She is currently chair of the brilliant team of hard-working geeks that form the Sci-Fi on the Rock committee.

Her following short story, *Hag Ridden*, first appeared in *Sci-Fi from the Rock Returns*.

Hag Ridden

Something's very wrong.
No, it's fine. Everything is good.
You're right. Everything's perfect.
The start:

It was a cold grey day with still air, the snowflakes falling straight down for a change. She and Rachel were playing in the wet snow. It was perfect for snowballs, snowmen, and forts. The yard was trampled, bare patches showing yellow grass, and here and there heaped walls of snow delineated hallways and rooms, decorated with sculpted furniture that had an icy finish from the warmth of their hands through gloves and mittens.

They were dishevelled but happy, laughing out clouds of warm breath. The blue shadows on the snow were dark and long, and it was time to head inside and warm up, to change into pyjamas and bathrobes and make hot chocolate with little pink and green marshmallows. But first, they paused: heads tilted back, tongues out to catch the giant fluffy flakes drifting down. Jennifer let her daughter think she won the race. But as the flake she caught melted on her tongue, she was shocked by an acrid taste. It was so sharp she almost gagged, but it dissipated after a second or two. As she followed Rachel inside, she wondered briefly what might have formed the unpleasant heart of the crystal.

Later:

The maps she had weren't detailed enough. Even online, the area she was interested in was chunky, pixelated. She dug out her alumni card and spent all afternoon at the map library, pulling out and discarding one satellite image after another. One sheet showed an area that came right to the edge of what she was looking for, but there was no adjoining photograph. She left still agitated, ignoring the black looks from the two staff members who had offered their help earlier and now felt resigned annoyance at the sight of the scattered and disorganized maps she had left in her wake.

To her husband and daughter, she seemed strangely distant and preoccupied. Jennifer was not herself. She did not seem to perceive this, however. When Ryan tried to talk to her about it, she was effortlessly evasive. She did not appear to be hiding anything, he concluded. She really believed there was nothing about her behaviour that was worth noting. She looked ill, with her dull hair and eyes, her skin gone sallow, her body seeming to lose definition with each passing day. But every morning she arranged her hair, applied her simple makeup, and saw her family off to school and to work before heading to her sunlit studio. She'd stopped painting the wildflowers she was known for. Her works were now larger, darker, and more abstract. What he saw of them showed shadowed woods, the gleam of a lake or pond. The careful detail so fundamental to her style was gone. The paintings had a dynamic, frenzied quality. He did not know who to call about this, about her. Rachel watched her mother with sorrowful eyes, uncomprehending and fearful. Mom says she's fine, but she's not. She's not.

When he returned from work one evening in spring, determined at last to take her to their doctor no matter what she said, she was gone.

She'd decided to go for a little drive on this fine fresh day. She didn't take much, just a canvas grocery bag of food she collected from the cupboards and fridge, a case of water, her comb, and her purse. There was a spot she'd been meaning to visit, and it wouldn't take long. She just knew she was going to love it. The desire had really hit her this morning. She'd been looking in the mirror, combing her hair, and she'd felt a surge of wrongness. Her eyes were sunken and ringed with bruised-looking skin, her hair littering the sink, and the bones of her face thrown into prominence by the too-bright light above the mirror. She was aghast at how thin and haggard she suddenly appeared. Moments ago she had looked as she always had, and now, so wretched. There was a twisting in her gut and she clutched at her distended belly. As it shifted under her fingers, her mind was thrown back to the first time she had felt Rachel kick. But this was not like that at all, and as she opened her mouth to gasp, to scream, she saw something move in the back of her throat: tendrils. The gleam of light caught on something like a claw; the choking slick sliding down her throat and into her chest and stomach and guts. Her eyes stared in terror and revulsion and ---

Everything is just fine, it's all ok.

  -- Her skin and hair perfect and smooth, eyes sparkling. Just a little lip-gloss and she'd be ready to go on that road trip she'd been thinking about for months. The grove. The lake. She just knew it would be exactly what she needed.

She followed the road as far as she could. She didn't even notice the worry on the face of the lady at the last gas station as she paid to fill the tank earlier. She'd almost didn't make it; her car had been running on fumes. It had been very uncomfortable. The anxiety was almost unbearable, yet once she had spotted the station the relief was immediate. Her face was tear-streaked and pitiful to behold when she handed over her debit card. She was not entirely calm, however. The need to reach the lake was insistent now. The woman asked her if she was okay. Did she need some help? She was fine. What a lovely spring afternoon. Everything's fine. Thank you so much.

The road was just dirt, there at the end. The lake was south through the woods. No trail really, at least not for someone her size. It was slow-going, and the anxiety was surging back. Crawling was faster, below the larger branches of the pines. The undergrowth was thick though, and she lost some skin and left some blood on the moss and ferns and dead trees in her path. The clearing, and the lake beyond was just as she imagined it. Or was it just as she remembered? The water was choppy even in the calm air, late afternoon sunlight catching the spray. She fought her way to her feet, stumbling towards the beautiful, perfect, intoxicating water.

Home: where she had always wanted to be.

At the shore, the pain caught her, surged through her. She stumbled, collapsed to her knees again. She suddenly felt everything - the raw and scraped skin of her hands and knees, the lacerations from the branches, a deep ache in her bones, her eyes burning, her joints throbbing in agony. Everything was wrong, and the worst of it turned in her gut, rose to be born on the shore of this dark and restless lake. She gagged and choked. No breath was possible as her rider, her commanding parasite, surged up her throat, filled her mouth and poured forth, seemingly endlessly onto the barren shore. It was slick with a vile grey slime, its taste acrid like that long ago snowflake. It had grown these past few months, plump and long, feeding on her flesh, filling her with longing for this churning, maggot-filled lake.

She watched so many grey and mottled bodies, sliding and twisting just under the surface. Her master rolled and slid its way to the edge, the tentacles that fringe its head lashing, reaching for the water. She reached too; her bloody skeletal hand tried to grasp it, to stop it, to punish it because she remembered now. Without it in her mind, she remembered Ryan and Rachel, their attempts to help her, her cheerful denials. She remembered the suppressed pain, the savage urge that compelled her to leave them, her despair buried under this beast's iron control. The long months of madness clumsily masked with the facade of normalcy. But she was weak, and her clutching fingers merely left shallow tracks in its coat of slime as it slips into the water, losing itself in the welcoming press of its fellows. Her head dropped and she looked along the shoreline, littered with the bones of countless animals, large and small, that dragged themselves and their remorseless cargo to the shore. Here and there, the curve of a human skull gleamed in the murk. She thought of Rachel and cold snow and that bitter snowflake as she closed her eyes.

Scott Bartlett

Scott Bartlett was born in St. John's, Newfoundland, where he lives. He is a fiction author who mostly writes science fiction nowadays, though he's dabbled in humor and literary fiction. He is a regular presence at Sci-Fi on the Rock.

The author's medieval comedy novel, *Royal Flush*, won the H. R. (Bill) Percy Prize, and his contemporary novel *Taking Stock*, about a young writer struggling with depression, won the Percy Janes First Novel Award, as well as the Lawrence Jackson Writers Award. Taking Stock was also a semi-finalist in the 2014 Best Kindle Book Awards.

Scott recently caught the sci-fi bug, and he's writing new novels at light speed. He especially enjoys writing dystopian sci-fi. The following is a short excerpt from his upcoming novel, *Flight From Dodge*.

Flight From Dodge
CHAPTER ONE

If Carl Intoever were to name the most important experience of his adolescence, he would probably have to go
with the day they told him he was the Messiah.

"God," the preacher told his congregation that Monday, "may or may not condone premarital sex. If there is
a God."

The congregation murmured.

"Avoiding sex before marriage—maybe that's a good
idea. It might limit the spread of STIs, and could mean
fewer children with uncertain familial situations. But does
God have an opinion on the matter? We don't know. We
can't know."

"We can't know," the congregation repeated in unison.

"It could be God really doesn't like it. Could be! It's
possible that if you do it, you'll be punished for it after
death. Maybe your fingernails will get plucked out, one
by one, by a demon wielding rusty pliers. Maybe you'll
be gored over and over by a unicorn!" The preacher
shrugged. "But maybe not. I really have no idea."

Fourteen-year-old Carl Intoever didn't have any idea,

either. Right now his main concern involved complying with Probablism orthodoxy as closely as possible so he wouldn't have to stay behind after Monday School for additional programming. He chimed in with the rest of the congregation whenever the preacher's rote call demanded a rote response, and otherwise he sat quietly and contemplated the unanswerable question of whether life could be said to have meaning, and whether one should bother getting out of bed on any given morning.

He'd been kept behind for additional programming before, and ultimately it amounted to having less time to don his gaming headset and lose himself in his favourite digital fantasies. Other than attend school and go to church, as his father required, video games filled his days. There wasn't much else for someone his age to do in Dodge. Most public spaces used a machine that emitted a high-pitched whine, which only teenagers could hear. Carl couldn't stand it for more than a couple minutes. Not so within the world of his headset: he was the hero there, and nothing good could happen without him. He wasn't hated, feared, or worse, ignored by society inside his video games.

When the sermon ended and all the youth lined up to exit through the rear and proceed down into the basement for Monday School Carl joined in, arranging himself for maximum inconspicuousness. Once downstairs, he headed for a seat in the classroom's middle.

"Probablism is the most evolved religion," the teacher told them once they were sitting. "That's why it's still around. Can anyone tell me what natural selection did to the other religions?"

Briefly, Carl considered putting up his hand. Never answering a question was a sure sign one needed additional programming. But before he could, Gregory Stronger's hand shot into the air, two rows in front of Carl.

"They were too unyielding in their doctrines, and agnosticism subverted them. Nothing is certain."

Carl breathed a sigh of relief. The answer he'd been considering paled beside Gregory's, and was probably wrong. Gregory made a practice of constantly one-upping Carl, in church, in school, even in online games. Carl gave silent thanks that at least this time the humiliation wasn't public.

"Very good, Gregory. People eventually realized the dominant religions of the day were making claims with insufficient evidence. And whenever evidence did come to light—such as the Earth turning out to revolve around the sun—the claims toppled." The teacher took a sip of water. "But the Probablist doctrine is built on agnosticism. We recognize nothing is certain, as Gregory said."

The preacher's shadow darkened the doorway. The teacher noticed, and fell silent. They all waited for the preacher to speak.

"Carl Intoever."

Carl stood, his chair scraping noisily against the floor amidst the silence. The preacher pointed a bony finger at him, and he shifted his weight from one foot to the other nervously. "I summon you to my chambers," the preacher said.

Making his way through the sea of chairs, Carl tried to remember whether he'd committed any spectacularly unorthodox acts lately. Why else would the preacher want to speak with him? Maybe the Monday School teacher thought additional programming would be a waste of time in his case, and had recommended extraordinary measures. What if they kept him for the rest of the day?

He followed the preacher out of the classroom and through the pristine corridor—past the statue of the pasta-creature, and past the portrait of the invisible unicorn (the canvas was blank). The preacher spoke. "Do you know why we're called preachers, and not priests, Carl?"

Carl cleared his throat, to buy time. "Um," he said. "Oh! Because that title would carry unseemly connotations of certainty."

The preacher turned his head to smile at him. "I'm beginning to see why you were chosen."

Carl's forehead wrinkled in confusion. "Ch-chosen?"

The preacher tittered. "Patience, Ward!" They had arrived. He pushed the door open. "Enter. Have a seat."

Carl sat before the giant desk, and the preacher sank into the lush armchair behind it, producing a large bottle of hand cream and squirting it liberally into his palm. He began rubbing it into his hands and arms.

"What I am about to tell you, you must share with no one."

Carl shifted in his seat. "Okay."

"Are you ready?" The preacher continued wringing his hands.

"I think so."

The preacher smiled. "You, Carl Intoever, are Schrödinger reborn. The Messiah."

For that, Carl had no words. The silence stretched on. Finally he said, "But Guardian, surely you mean I might be—"

"No. Of everything in the universe, this one thing is certain. You are destined to someday deliver humankind unto salvation. You will save us, Carl Intoever."

Carl breathed. "Wow."

"I know," the preacher said, nodding. "It's a lot to take in. Run along, then."

Carl stood, but hesitated before leaving. "Um, so—what do I do?"

The preacher raised his eyebrows. "Oh, you'll know in time. You'll just know." His brow furrowed. "It might take a while."

Carl nodded, and left the preacher's office. Monday School had ended, and the other youth filled the corridors. A few glanced at him with curiosity.

He returned their looks, and found that he was fighting to suppress a grin.

Somehow, he had suspected this all along.

CHAPTER TWO

Twenty-eight-year-old Carl Intoever peeled off the blankets and willed his limbs to stir. He wanted them to propel his torso, catlike, over Maria, without waking her. They wouldn't, though. He suspected they were in secret conversation with his brain, which didn't wish to start the day even a little.

Finally he managed to heave his mass up and to the right. He didn't quite make it to the floor. He landed partially on Maria, who squawked, and beat him savagely with her pillow. Something loosened inside his bowels, and he ran for the washroom. "Don't know why you must have that side, anyhow!" he shouted back at her as he ran. Maria got up much later than him, and he could do without this part of the morning ritual. She should be the one to sleep against the wall.

Not long after he'd unlaced his pyjamas and eased himself onto the seat, the wall before him turned on, displaying a white background with black text:

"HAVING A SHIT ARE WE"

Carl sighed. He'd spent the better part of last night bolstering the house's firewall. It didn't matter, of course. The hackers always found a way in. This one was probably some geezer—his best defenses would be laughable, to a geezer.

The text dissolved, and another message replaced it: "YOU'RE LOOKING PARTICULARLY SPOTTY TODAY, CARL. DID YOU KNOW THAT?"

"Bugger off."

"YOU'RE A VERY UGLY MAN"

Given his status as the Messiah, Carl found adulthood surprisingly dreary and aggravating. Nothing about his life suggested he was special, and so no one could discern his divine origins other than him. He wanted to be a good person and to help people, which he assumed would contribute to fulfilling his holy mandate, but he didn't see how anyone could manage it while still living in Dodge, where success typically required a lot of nastiness.

He'd recently concluded that his destiny had to be waiting for him in the New World, where, according to the tourist videos, society wasn't set up to incentivize bad behaviour. Most everyone in Dodge spent their adult lives saving money for a one-way airplane ticket to the New World, and Carl was no exception. Until he got there, he would simply have to put being a good person on the back burner.

Right now, all he wanted was to get to work without feeling like a complete piece of shit.

He finished up in the washroom and stumble into the kitchen for his daily omelette. As he took out a frying pan, the wall behind the sink came alive. "THERE AREN'T ANY EGGS, CARL. I'VE ALREADY CHECKED."

Carl opened the fridge to verify that claim. "Bugger," he muttered. Sighing, he put away the pan.

He returned to the bathroom to brush his teeth. His toothbrush chimed when he laid it down again; signalling it had registered the amount of toothpaste used and transmitted it to be logged on his public consumption record.

As always, his briefcase awaited him in the porch. He laced up his boots and reached for the access pole to slide down into the ground-level lobby—homes were designed this way to keep them above the frequent flooding. As his fingers touched the pole, the wall before him became a screen displaying more text. Something perverse inside made him stop and read it.

"YOU'RE A DETRIMENT TO THE SPECIES, CARL...A PROPER EUGENICS PROGRAM WOULD HAVE PREVENTED YOU FROM EVER EXISTING."

A Messiah is destined to suffer—Carl knew that. Even so, this was a bit much.

He slid down the pole into the vast lobby. As he did, he realized he'd forgotten to apply NanoSpray. Today would be the day he got skin cancer, he didn't doubt it.

Gregory Stronger was walking by as he landed, and a smile sprung automatically to Carl's lips. Encountering Gregory this early suggested grim things about how well his day would go, but Gregory was currently his senior at work, which meant the brownnosing would now commence. Carl hated brownnosers, but he hated his life even more, and escaping it meant taking opportunities where he could get them. There was always the possibility Gregory could get his contract extended.

"Good morning, Gregory!" he said.

"Morning, Carl." Gregory had been thumbing his phone, and Carl's presence certainly didn't cause him to stop. "How might things be?"

"Oh, well, you know. I've got hackers again."

Gregory sniffed. "I paid a geezer in accounting to set up my security. Haven't had hackers since."

"Brilliant! You'll have to refer me." Which was bollocks, of course. He couldn't afford that, and they both knew it. "Are we still on for drinks, Thursday? Six-thirty, did we say?"

Gregory considered this for a moment. "I'd estimate a seventy-one percent probability I'll be there."

Carl suppressed a frown. Making plans with a devout Probablist was perhaps the most frustrating exercise ever. "Brilliant," he said.

They walked through the dimly lit lobby in silence, weaving through the forest of access poles. Every now and then a resident would slide down one, and everyone below had to take care they weren't landed on. It took Carl and Gregory ten minutes to reach the exit, and by then they were most of the way to work.

They watched through the window as a strong gust blew the raindrops horizontally against the glass.

"I'll hail a taxi," Gregory said. "You can ride for free, if you like."

Carl didn't trust that. To offer him a free ride meant Gregory wanted something.

But he accepted the ride. What else could he do?

CHAPTER THREE

Judging from his morning, Carl's day was shaping up like any other: disappointing and dehumanizing. He could almost see a parade of identical days, stretching to the horizon. The only escape lay in embracing the drudgery and working hard, the sooner to buy a plane ticket from Air Earth and get out of Dodge. To that end, he sent Maria a text as soon as he got to his workstation: "you gonna look for jobs today?"

His own contract ended soon, and he didn't expect it to be renewed. He spent most of his free time searching for another. Unfortunately the same couldn't be said of Maria, who five minutes later still hadn't answered his text.

He sent another: "I'm counting on you. We'll never get to the new world unless we both pull our weight"

He glanced up from his phone. Brenda strolled by his workstation. The words "A responsible resident of both air and earth" were currently emblazoned across her smartshirt, underneath the logo for Air Earth. "Hi, Carl," she said, wearing a warm smile.

"Hi, Brenda." His gaze lingered on her as she passed,

remaining focused on her chest until he realized what he was doing. "Shit," he muttered under his breath. That had probably been a bad idea. Maria had access to his lifelog, and if she happened to watch that part, he would be in for it.

For a moment Carl considered whether he should break things off with Maria in order to find someone self-motivated like Brenda, who was extremely orthodox and who worked hard to afford a plane ticket out of Dodge. But he quickly scrapped the notion. Because of her strict orthodoxy he likely wouldn't be able to stand Brenda. Part of why he'd initially been attracted to Maria was her disinterest in participating properly in society.

He threw himself into his work, in the hopes that management would notice and extend his contract. His work consisted of fielding email complaints from social network users whose posts had been removed. Carl's current contract was with Safetalk, a firm that corporations paid to safeguard their brands. Safetalk had an arrangement with Unfurl, the dominant social network, whereby bots scanned the millions of hourly posts for ones that violated the trademarks of Safetalk clients. The bots automatically removed the infringing ones. Users normally found this upsetting.

Such as the one whose complaint Carl reviewed now. "This is bullshit," the user wrote. "My friend referenced CabLab last week, in almost exactly the same way I did. Why was my post taken down and hers wasn't?"

The user had provided a link to his friend's post, and Carl clicked it. It turned out the friend had praised CabLab, while the complainer's post had criticized the company.

In cases like this one, it used to be Safetalk policy to try and distinguish between two such posts, explaining why the complainer's post was infringing while the friend's was not. That had required a lot of effort, though, and also exposed Safetalk to liability, since it was committing to a specific interpretation of trademark law that it could be called on to defend in court.

"Oops!" Carl wrote in his reply to the user. "Your friend's post must have slipped through our filters. I will ensure hers is deleted as well. Thank you for bringing this additional violation to our attention!"

As promised, Carl deleted the friend's post, and then sent her a message crediting the complainer with notifying Safetalk that she had violated CabLab's trademark. As a result, she would likely send the complainer a message like this: "Thanks a lot for getting my post deleted, asshole." She might even make a public post about it, shaming him for his snitching. He would probably never complain to Safetalk again.

This approach had, in fact, been Carl's innovation, for which he'd received zero acknowledgment from his superiors. This was the way of things: you worked a contract as cheerfully as possible, and during it, whatever company happened to be employing you took credit for any ideas you might have. If the company decided your usefulness had expired before your contract end date, a manager would come and suggest you break off the contract. That would look bad on your record, but the dirt they'd dig up should you refuse to leave would look even worse.

All this served to explain the level of shock he experienced when his boss, Morrowne, called him to his office and gave him a promotion.

That happened after lunch. Morrowne sat behind his desk, his belly straining against it, and a man with whom Carl wasn't acquainted rested in a plush recliner off to the side. Morrowne puffed on a noncarcinogenic cigar clamped between his ample lips.

"Mr. Morrowne," Carl said. "Good afternoon."

Morrowne was a geezer, which was uncommon for anyone wealthy—most people purchased an airplane ticket long before they accumulated as much money as Morrowne had.

"Intoever," Morrowne said, "This is Xavier Ofvalour."

Carl glanced at the man in the recliner. "No, it's not," he said.

The man raised his eyebrows, and Morrowne said, "Excuse me?"

Carl looked again, and his heart rate tripled. "Schrödinger's cat! It really is, isn't it?"

"It really is," Xavier Ofvalour said.

Xavier Ofvalour was the most successful man in all of Dodge: strong, shrewd, and (as a direct consequence) rich. This made him revered. Famous, of course. A thrill-seeking mastermind, he could squeeze money from a turnip, or so it was said. And he occupied the top spot on the LifeRank leaderboard, a rank that conferred the title Hand of the Market.

"I apologize, Mr. Ofvalour," Carl said. "My worldview didn't accommodate us ever meeting—I need to make some quick adjustments to it—I didn't mean to deny you.

That was rude of me, Mr. Ofvalour, and no offense was meant."

"You have a strange way of talking."

"But rest assured," Morrowne said. "He's the best in his department."

Carl raised his eyebrows. He felt overwhelmed by this torrent of recognition.

"Well," Xavier Ofvalour said, "fine. But it's not enough for me to know he's the best—I must know why. What makes you so good at what you do, Mr. Intoever?"

Morrowne's brow furrowed. "You've seen his Work-Stars profile, haven't you? Five-star ratings, pretty much across the board. Did you read the reviews?"

"I asked Mr. Intoever a question, Morrowne."

"I'm good because I hate it," Carl said. "I hate this job, just like I hated every job I've ever taken. I hate my life, too. It's my hatred that motivates me to take more jobs, and to excel at them, because the harder I work, the quicker I can leave Dodge forever."

"Yes," Xavier Ofvalour said. "But everyone hates life here, don't they? If we're speaking frankly."

"Well, let's not—" Morrowne began, but Xavier Ofvalour silenced him with a gesture.

"We all know of your sacrifice, Mr. Morrowne. It's identical to mine. We remain in Dodge to perform the necessary administrative work. Someone's got to do it, and anyway we're lavishly rewarded. But I'm still curious about Mr. Intoever's effectiveness. Are you suggesting, Mr. Intoever, that you have an above-average hatred for your life? Are you saying you hate your life with uncommon verve?"

"Yes," Carl said. "In essence."

"Very well, then. Tell him what I want, Mr. Morrowne."

Morrowne cleared his throat. "Mr. Ofvalour has acquired FutureBrite, a residential youth care company."

Carl opened his mouth to speak, but closed it again. He glanced at Xavier Ofvalour, whose expression was neutral. "Ah," Carl said.

"Yes. I'm sure you're aware of the attendant controversies. Busybodies calling them 'kid farms', claiming they place profit before the children." Morrowne spread his hands. "But what's the alternative? A government-run organization?"

"We'd need to establish a government for that," Xavier Ofvalour said, and they all shared a laugh, even Carl.

"Anyhow," Morrowne said. "Mr. Ofvalour is under heavy fire on the networks for his acquisition—too much for us to address using Safetalk's current infrastructure. Which is why he's commissioning the creation of an entirely new department, devoted solely to protecting youth care brands. Certainly, it will focus almost entirely on FutureBrite, but no one need know that."

"My girlfriend probably already knows, though," Carl said. "She has access to my lifelog, and monitors it frequently. And my insurance company—"

"Don't be daft," Xavier Ofvalour said. "Your lifefeed paused the moment you entered the office."

"Of course," Carl said. Maria wouldn't like that.

"We're calling it the Youth Dignity Department," Morrowne said. "We need someone to head it. And check your scruples at the door, Intoever—you won't get an opportunity like this again."

Carl blinked. "You're—you're choosing me?"

Morrowne exchanged glances with Xavier Ofvalour. "Did I stutter?"

"No, sir," Carl said. "And rest assured—" He patted his pockets. "—no scruples here! Did I mention how much I hate my life?" He gave a nervous laugh, but this time he laughed alone.

"Perform this task well, and you'll be out of Dodge before you know it," Xavier Ofvalour said. "I doubt you'll need to sign another contract again."

"I'll do it," Carl said. He found the prospect of escaping Dodge sooner than he'd projected thoroughly exciting.

"Of course you will," Morrowne said, exchanging glances with Xavier Ofvalour as he cleared his throat. "Should we let Intoever know about the other reason for creating the department?"

Xavier Ofvalour nodded. "It's best for him to be fully informed."

"Very well. A big reason we're doing this, Intoever, is that a week ago someone stole two-hundred thousand sensitive documents from FutureBrite's private servers. We don't yet know who did it, but we do know that only an employee of the company could have that kind of access. We suspect whoever took the documents is looking for a way to release them that won't be suppressed. So it's our job to ensure no such platform exists, while keeping FutureBrite's reputation as spotless as possible, to shelter it against the enormous risk posed by these leaks."

"What was in these documents?" Carl asked carefully.

"Damning stuff," Xavier Ofvalour said. "Damning enough to sink the company. And that's all you need to know."

"Understood."

"Take the rest of the day off, Intoever," Morrowne said. "It would be proper to celebrate with your significant other. Tomorrow you'll begin your new position."

"Thank you, Mr. Morrowne. Thank you, Mr. Ofvalour."

"Don't disappoint," Xavier Ofvalour said as Carl left the office.

Gathering his things from his workstation, Carl decided that most of all, this felt like vindication. He'd always known, being Schrödinger reborn, that he was destined for great things. But he'd been waiting a long time, and he'd suffered enough for ten messiahs. Could his work defending Xavier Ofvalour's new initiative tie in somehow with the divine duty Carl was destined to perform?

Probably not, he decided, remembering what Morrowne said about checking his scruples. Whatever destiny had in store for Carl as Messiah, it probably involved scruples. But at the very least this new position would help him get to the actual 'being a good person' part a lot sooner.

Jay Paulin

Jay Paulin was born and raised in Southwestern Ontario. From the time he could put crayon to paper, he wanted to be a storyteller. His first project was a dinosaur puppet show that earned rave reviews from his stuffed animals.

In the mid-2000's, Paulin settled in Nova Scotia, where Ink'd Well Comics burst into existence. Since then, Ink'd Well Comics has evolved into a small press, releasing print and web comics, and providing others an outlet for their own ideas. The brand is perhaps best known for their charity anthologies that shine a spotlight on independent creators. The three collections have raised thousands of dollars for both Child's Play and Free The Children. In addition to appearing at many conventions across Canada, Paulin has become a regular at Sci-Fi on the Rock, participating in a variety of writing and publishing related panels.

Aside from writing and reading, Paulin enjoys watching films, playing and watching sports, and playing and listening to music. Most of all, he enjoys being a goofy dad to his young daughter.

The following story is a prose piece set in the same world as his hit comic series *Super Galactic Space Explorers*.

Spooky's Gambit:
A *Super Galactic Space Explorers* Tail

"Aiiieeeeeee!"

Cadet Meatball yowled in Commander Spooky's ears, adding to the noise from the warning buzzers and alarms.

"Cut it out back there and help me get the shields back up!" the commander ordered.

This was Spooky's first assignment since her promotion, and it wasn't going as well as planned.

THOOM.

The small standard-issue two-cat shuttle of the Super Galactic Space Explorers wasn't made for space battles, and each successful strike was a harsh reminder of this fact. The S.G.S.E. are an agency dedicated to discovery, and peace. What the two explorers discovered on this seemingly straightforward mission was anything but peaceful.

With a click, Spooky managed to redirect the power to the rear shields moments before another blast hit the ship. "That was too close," she sighed over a dull hum.

"We're not out of it yet," Meatball groaned. "Why did you get us into this mess? Commander Boots never would have crossed paths with pirates." Spooky shrunk a bit in her seat at the sound of her friend and mentor's name. Boots was the best the S.G.S.E. had to offer, and had volunteered to take Meatball out on a diplomatic visit. Still recovering from an injury suffered during the war against Queen KitKat, Boots nevertheless put the needs of others first. Spooky convinced Boots to stay behind, and then was assigned a new recruit."

Are your missions always like this? The commander is stuck pushing papers because of your--"

THOOM.

Spooky had no time to respond to the cadet's goading. Their shields were down again. One more blast and the duo would be doomed.

"Can you see how many are on our back?" Spooky asked, as she hastily manipulated the ship's control systems. Unfortunately for her, Meatball wasn't a lean cat, and he was only able to wiggle in his seat for brief moment.

"Uh... it's too dark," the cadet sheepishly replied. He looked at the dead control panel in front of him. Forgetting momentarily about Spooky in the lead seat, he banged the screen in front of him.

"Hey!" Spooky yelped, mostly out of surprise. Meatball ignored her, and began to grin as a faint light appeared before his eyes.

"We've got something! Three... no, four small fighters. That's not counting the big one." Meatball's voice trailed off a bit toward the end, remembering that raiders tend to travel in packs, and that the leader rarely gets his or her paws dirty.

Spooky solemnly nodded, as if reading her student's mind. "Then we don't have many options."

The commander opened a customized hatch that she had cut into the main panel herself. Inside was another of Spooky's patented creations. "Hold on. This is going to get a bit bumpy." She pressed a button on a makeshift box, and then clenched onto the steering column tightly. A bluish-yellow flame burst from the rear of the ship, and the explorers began to spiral downward in the direction of a nearby moon.

"We got 'em!" a pirate cheered. The others began whooping through the intercom, before static and fury interrupted the celebration.

"Idiots," a deep voice hissed. "Mere flares, disguised to fool only the stupidest of enemies." King growled to himself, but the act intimidated the crew on his deck. They all sat a little straighter, and they pulled levers with 20% more efficiency. "I must admit," he continued, "a decent ruse. After we kill them, I want to inspect their ship personally before you strip it down."

"Yes, sir!" the pirates responded in unison. Last week, one pirate was a bit slow to agree, and he was kicked out of the garbage bay doors into space. Nobody wanted to anger their boss a second time.

It has been nearly two months since the war with Queen KitKat ended, and Princess Missy signed a peace accord with the Super Galactic Space Explorers. Electing to live a lavish lifestyle, she dismissed all but the most attractive soldiers, and mostly disappeared off the grid. The majority of the troops went back to whatever duties they performed in their civilian lives, but the rest had a taste for battle. For glory. For blood.

Privateers popped up, hitting places that were already weakened by the war. The S.G.S.E., trained but not built for extensive battling, were stretched thin. Between aiding planets, rebuilding their ranks, and returning to standard duties, they were not always able to fight off the marauders. Then there were the seedier worlds distrustful of the explorers even before the war. It made sense for them to join, or at least support, the space gangs.

King's crew, The Untamables, was one of the nastiest of all the buccaneers. The soldiers were part of Kit-Kat's Shock and Claw squadron, and trained to be merciless machines of war. The ships were scavenged from the wreckage, and often coloured to mislead authorities. King would strike an area with one set of ships, then swoop in with another and offer 'protection' in exchange for money and supplies. After gaining trust, discovering the location of the valuables, and determining the difficulty of seizing all assets, The Untamables would touch down and take over.

This was becoming an all-too-common occurrence in the post-war galaxy.

Today, King and company were scouting a new site when the S.G.S.E.'s blue and gold ship came on the scene. Knowing the reputation boost that would accompany the capture of an explorer or two, he wasted little time in announcing The Untamables' presence.

Despite recognizing that his target's ship was not destroyed, at least due to his pirates, he believed a technique would never be used unless in case of emergency. Success was so close that he could taste it. King smiled as his man-of-war class vessel, the *Indominus*, began its descent toward the moon. This was shaping up to be a very good day.

This was shaping up to be a very bad day. Cadet Meatball's grumbling had not ceased, from the moment the duo crash-landed, to now as they navigated the wilderness. Even Commander Spooky's happy-go-lucky demeanor was being tested. The two explorers continued deeper, however, because uncertain death in front of them sure beat certain death behind them.

As if on cue, the two heard the unmistakable sound of ship exhausts whirring down. They decided to hasten their escape.

"I bet Commander Boots never got lost on a strange world," Meatball muttered. He noticed Spooky looking in his direction, and smirked. "Well, aside from the time she was with you."

"Every explorer has faced danger, and will continue to face danger," Spooky explained, almost as if repeating a mantra. "It is part of our job, and we will do it with pride."

"Oh, I'm not saying I don't want to face danger," Meatball said as he cut through a series of thick vines. "I just wish it wasn't today."

For the first time all day, Spooky smiled at one of his jabs. "Me, too."

King stood on the shore of a large lake, his back to the handful of crewmembers that unloaded weapons from the *Indominus*. Instead, he watched as a few more of his pirates used winches and cables to pull the S.G.S.E. wreck from the water. Despite the crash landing, the ship was in remarkably good shape. It was then that King noticed the submersible retrofitting. He began to chuckle, and thought, *Maybe these explorers are smarter than I thought.*

"All set, sir!" King's concentration was broken, but he didn't mind. It was time he squashed the two pests before they had a chance to call some friends.

King walked over toward the pile of blasters. One of his buccaneers, a strapping fellow, picked up a large rock, then threw it into the jungle. "Ow! What the?"

The raiders sniggered, even their leader, until a laser blast shot out from between the trees and dropped the stone thrower. King doubled over with laughter, and seeing his reaction, the others let their guard down and joined him. Suddenly, King stood up seemingly larger than ever. He roared, and yelled, "Kill them!"

"Nice shot!" Commander Spooky sputtered between gasps. As soon as Cadet Meatball, a surprisingly crack shot, fired toward the origin of the stone, the two took off running.

"T-t-thanks!" the younger cat said. He was too exhausted to be snarky. All of his focus was on running, an action his body was simply not built for. "Wh-w-w-

wheeze"

Spooky interrupted with a soft solemn voice that could barely be heard over the aggressive stomps of feet growing louder by the second. "We survive."

Commander Spooky wasn't just a genius with ships, but she was also adept at creating gadgets of any kind. She was a bit of a scaredy-cat normally, but carved out her own place due to her ability to subdue and distract, allowing her to escape to safety. Unfortunately for Spooky and Meatball, this was supposed to be a simple mission. As such, her utility belt was a bit lighter than usual. Nonetheless, she fiddled and combined, trusting her cadet to keep the path clear ahead whenever she needed to look down.

"It's getting thicker! I *huff* don't think I can keep cutting alone." Meatball sliced through a cluster of branches, and then looked over his shoulder. "You listening?"

Spooky attached a few springs to some flexible metal, then tossed them blindly over her shoulder. "Yes," she huffed. "But you're going to have to." Never stopping for a moment, the freshly minted commander continued to alternate between dropping odd discs and tossing the improvised snares.

A chorus of "Oof!" and yelps echoed amongst the trees and vines. Spooky grinned. *If a few are stopped, the better our odds will be.*

The two cats hurdled a fallen log, then the leader held up a paw to signal a pause. "Crouch here," she instructed.

"Why?"

Spooky cupped her hands around her mouth, and let out a booming howl. "Aaaaarooooooooo!"

"You crazy cat, you're going to get us killed!" Meatball yelled in a whispered voice, and he tried shaking sense into his partner.

Spooky stared into the distance, and softly admitted, "Something I learned from... from a friend. Now come on." She crouched, and began weaving through the plant life. Space was opening up between the foliage, and more light was peeking through. The commander was certain there was a clearing ahead. Hopefully the raiders fell for yet another of her desperate measures.

"Get back here! Now!"

The pirates couldn't escape quickly enough. They were stepping on one another, running straight into trees, and generally overreacting.

"Monster! Beast! Cat-eater!" they all screamed. The buccaneer leader sneered, and shot the loudest, most cowardly of the bunch. Some of the cats immediately snapped back to their senses. King of the Untamables disposed of the ones that didn't.

"Let's finish this," he snarled. Trudging forward, his group of eight became seven, then six, and then five.

One particularly dumb pirate pointed out the obvious. "Booby traps!"

King growled. "If I had these two explorers in my crew, I'd have mopped the floor with all of you."

The dumb pirate looked ashamed for a brief moment, until he stepped on one of Spooky's snare traps. King didn't even look in the direction of his pirate to notice the cat was crumpled in the mud, and posed like a pretzel.

The ever-shrinking group approached a fallen log. King scratched his chin, and then ordered one of his raiders to inspect.

"They definitely sat here. I think I know where they went."

King was happy to have one competent crewmember with him. "You come with me," the leader commanded. "And pick one to stay here in case they return."

Left behind, a young marauder whistled to pass the time. A gentle breeze wafted through, and he spotted something on the ground glimmering in the faint sunlight. Approaching it with caution, he suddenly stopped. "A coin?" He bent over to pick it up, only to trigger the last of Commander Spooky's traps.

"What's taking them so long?" whined Cadet Meatball. Spooky glared at him, hoping he'd realize precisely what he had said. Their eyes met, and the youngster got the hint.

"Just stay still, make sure your blaster is aimed, and..." Spooky became quiet. Her student began to ask, but then saw the reason for her silence. Not twenty feet from where they were hiding up in the trees, King and three buccaneers had entered the clearing.

"I had hoped I had stopped more of them," Spooky lamented.

"Well, I think you did a great job... Commander."

Spooky looked over at the severely overweight cat next to her. Whether the comment was fuelled by respect, guilt, or fear of the situation, it was a nice break from the earlier venom she had taken. She exhaled, and then aimed her blaster.

"May you always land on your feet, cadet."

"And you yours," Meatball replied, and then proceeded to down two pirates without hesitation.

Spooky dropped from the tree, and quickly switched to a prone position before firing on the last of King's marauders.

"You think that impresses me?" King yelled.

"I sure do!" Meatball replied. The cat then tried to leap down, but his weight caused a branch to snap, sending the youngster face down.

"Haw, haw, haw-haw!" King snorted. He had an obnoxious laugh, and Spooky felt a small amount of pity for his team of raiders that had to listen to it all day. She snapped out of it, remembering they were villains and got what they deserved.

"Thanks for your help, commander," Meatball sarcastically said as he dusted himself off. "Enjoy your daydream?"

Before Spooky had a chance to apologize, King's voice boomed again. "I have a proposal for you. I won't kill the both of you. In exchange, I will spare the clever one. The one who built all those gadgets."

Cadet Meatball gulped. "And the other?"

"Killed, of course. But not by me. Consider it a rite of initiation. Haw! Haw-haw!"

The student looked toward his teacher. "W-w-what do we--"

Spooky interrupted. "He built the devices. Take him."

King shrugged. "Whatever. Just one of you die already."

Commander Spooky nodded, and then kneeled. She asked her student to make it quick. One shot on the shield generator at her waist, and then one more to the chest. Meatball began to tear up, and sputtered, "Sh-sh-shield? You don't--"

Spooky looked up and smiled at the cadet, who finally understood.

In the blink of an eye, he fired. "Huh?" He fired again. "Yaarrrf." King dropped, and spoke no more.

Spooky stood up, and wiped the mud off of her knees. "Admiral Momo will be pleased." She looked at the young explorer, still coming to terms with the last 60 seconds. "Commander Boots, too."

Meatball continued to stand in silence. "What about you?"

Spooky walked over, extended her paw, and said, "I think you did an excellent job. Not all cadets are as calm and collected in danger."

Meatball blushed, and then went to shake her paw. He quickly pulled back, and then saluted. Spooky saluted back, and said, "Let's head home."

Erin Vance

Erin Vance is an editor and a graduate of the Memorial University of Newfoundland English Honours Program. Erin wrote her Honours thesis paper, *The Song of the Mockingjay*, as an exploration of the nature of Katniss Everdeen's agency in Suzanne Collins' *The Hunger Games* series. She is creative, spiritual, and loves reading, writing, and anything to do with words.

In 2015, Erin crossed Canada from coast to coast in a brief break from her continuing education. We are happy to report she returned to St. John's unscathed, much to the joy of her beautiful Newfoundland pups.

Erin was first published at age 17 as part of a poetry anthology, and is currently in the process of writing her first novel for Engen Books.

Cast, Clutter, Pack, Murder

You know your life is crap when you have to share your bedroom with about a dozen other animals.

Something nudged Vico's foot; he peered down to see a mangy dog nose at his sock. His (or hers. Its? Whatever) tail thumped on the floor upon noticing Vico's gaze on it. Vico frowned at the bald spot on its left hindquarters and felt something twang painfully in his chest.

"Don't even think about it," he croaked. He shoved at the dog half-heartedly with his foot. "Probably covered in fleas," he muttered.

Above his head, a pigeon cooed, and another answered it. Another dog whined from underneath Vico's cot, and a third scratched at the wall. Something swatted his forehead and he lifted his chin to see a large black cat sitting by his left ear, one paw still raised. One ear was mangled, chewed nearly in half, and its fur was matted in clumps. It swatted Vico's forehead again.

Vico scowled at the cat, but closed his eyes. Cats would do whatever the hell they wanted; best to leave them to it.

There was a thud above his head and a flurry of wings

flapping and a bird's squawk and the squeaking of rusting metal being forced to move. Some cat had jumped onto the pigeon cage again; a couple feathers landed on Vico's stomach. A dog let out another whine and another one barked twice. Vico swore under his breath and hunched his shoulders.

A low long beep sounded and then a voice said, "How are you, Mr. Baggio?"

Vico opened one eye and glared at the ceiling with it. "Peachy," he answered, only to be swatted by the cat again.

"Sarcasm does not become you, Mr. Baggio," the voice countered. It was female and human, although its cadence was slightly off in a way Vico couldn't describe. "We should be ready for you soon."

Vico opened the other eye and used his left hand to prop himself up. He dug his right elbow into the thin mattress for balance as he struggled to raise himself into an inclined position. "Finally," he groaned. "This place is a dump."

The mangy dog that had nosed his sock earlier whined as Vico struggled to sit up fully. It shifted positions, turning so it could rest its chin on Vico's right leg. Its chin was damp, and drool began to soak into his pants.

That twang vibrated in his chest again, and Vico scowled in compensation. "Dumb dog," he grumbled. "Can't you see I can't pet you?" After all, he didn't have an arm past his right elbow – just an ugly, red stump. Made it difficult to do much of anything, let alone give an abandoned dog a head scratch.

"That'll change shortly, Mr. Baggio," the voice said.

"*If* the surgery works," he countered, shooting the cat a dirty look as it slunk past him.

"It'll work," the voice said, rather mild for its conviction. "We have not spent the last three years in vain."

The dog beneath his cot chose that moment to shuffle out and pause at his right side, giving a full-body shake that forced Vico to turn his head away. The dog with its head on his lap whined again, and the black cat swatted at his left foot.

"The three human subjects previous to you have exceeded our original schematics," the voice continued. "I can now announce that we are ahead of schedule."

Vico raised an eyebrow even as he wiggled his foot away from the cat. "Wow, Miranda. You almost sound excited."

"I believe I'll gas you now," Miranda replied, voice still mild. "We have to maintain our secrets, you understand."

Vico watched as a white mist began to seep out of the walls, escaping from invisible vents about a foot off the ground. A dog began barking, the one on his left went back under the cot, the birds began flapping their wings, and a trio of cats began howling. "I hate you," he said evenly.

"I recommend lying back down, Mr. Baggio," Miranda said. "A concussion would be an unnecessary complication for our surgeons."

Vico swore again, but began the painful and slow process of reclining. The cat curled up by his foot, and the dog raised its chin off his leg only to place its front paws on the cot. Vico paused, half-reclined, and said, "No…"

The dog jumped up; if the cot hadn't been bolted to the floor, the three of them would have gone toppling to the floor. As it was, Vico was laid flat, the cat sat up and hissed, digging its claws into Vico's leg. He would have sworn except the dog had landed on his gut and all of his breath had escaped in a low *guh*. "Dammit," he wheezed.

"Don't worry, Mr. Baggio," Miranda said as the world began to grow fuzzy at the edges, the blur seeping into his vision like the gas seeped into the room. "You're in the hands of professionals."

The dog rested its head on the center of Vico's chest, and began creating a new damp patch.

Once upon a time, there was a war-

(and then another, and another, and another – or was it all just the next phase of that first one?)

-and some countries rallied together and some allied against, and a man who was not yet forty took his younger wife and his four children, and left his home. They fled their proud country still struggling to regain the glory they had held as the Roman Empire, and flew to that prouder country across the Atlantic. His only daughter and eldest son, despite their young age, remembered the smell of war, and the tension in the weeks leading up to their departure, and found freedom in the airship that took them across the sea. They remembered their old home, and found their new home lacking. They grew bitter and melancholy from their memories haunting them, and found they could neither settle roots nor stretch to the skies.

The eldest son grew up in-between wars – or in a calmer phase of that singular one – and joined the army for a cause he didn't believe in. But they gave him a gun and a purpose, and taught him how to fly, and that was worth the omnipresent taste of blood in his mouth.

He rose, both literally and metaphorically. He piloted a small airship called a Warnet – loathed the wordplay and loved the vessel itself. He captained four other men, and the aching in his chest began to settle and soothe, even as his hands grew stained brown with dried blood.

Then he found hell.

(He was raised a good Catholic boy; he knew what hell was: fire and brimstone and never-ending screams.)

He lost half of his arm, he lost his ship, and in the losing, lost the only things keeping him together.

Two years later, he crawled back to the people who had cost him the closest thing to happiness he ever knew, besides that of his old, Italian home. They promised him a new arm and a new ship and something better than a gun. He accepted the offer, because a bitter, poisoned something was better than the gaping nothingness haunting him now.

Did he find salvation? Only in the same way Noah's Ark was: a rocky journey from one kind of survival to another struggle of the same, all the while surrounded by animals and their waste.

He missed his gun.

He had ten fingers again; it didn't matter that five were gray and glass with wires and softly pulsating blue lights

– they were fingers that bent when he willed them too, and could reach out and pet that damn dog if he wanted.

"I see you've made a friend," Miranda said coolly, her eyes focused on the tablet in her hands.

Vico scratched the top of the dog's head and was rewarded with it closing its eyes. "Something like that," he said, eyes focused on the wires exposed where a diseased left leg had been, and a leg remarkably similar to his new right forearm was now. The other three legs gleamed silver in the artificial lights of the recovery room, and slowly pulsed blue light through the joint bulbs.

A soft *whump* sounded on his right, and he turned to see the large black cat paw at its cage weakly. Its mangled ear had been replaced with a silver one, with metal plating traveling down the right side of its face; its right eye was now laser-beam red.

"Of course, a secondary surgery will be performed in a week's time," Miranda continued. "The skin grafts are a much less complicated surgery, statistically speaking. There is only a 7% chance of rejection, and even then, we have not lost any subjects."

Vico glanced down at his hand, bent and straightened each new finger in turn. "Is the skin graft necessary?" he asked, voice quiet.

Miranda paused. "Objectively, no. Not in your case. However, all other human subjects have found psychological calm with the secondary surgery-"

"But I can refuse it?" he asked, turning on his heel. "Right?" he demanded, voice hard.

Miranda looked at him through her thick glasses. She was not a pretty woman, but she wasn't ugly either – her hair was neat but never styled, and her skin had the pale tint of someone who lacked Vitamin D. She was a little skinny, but Vico contributed that to the fact that he'd only seen her eat once, and that was while she was very distracted. Her face was average, her nose a little large, her ears a little small, and her lips pale pink. She was obviously female, but just as obviously lacked sex appeal.

"You may refuse the skin graft," she agreed, her voice calm. She looked down at her tablet and began swiping her finger across it. "Please be aware, however, that it will be noted on your psych analysis."

"Yeah, whatever," he said, turning back to the dog. He reached through the bars of the cage to scratch the dog's head again.

"We've programmed those two as your captains," Miranda said. "Seeing as you seemed to have developed a bond already."

Vico paused in his scratching. *Programmed.* He swallowed the sudden bile in his throat and focused on the other issue: "I thought I was gonna have an airship."

"That is true; however, your ship will host four platoons – two terrain and two aerial. These before you comprise 4% of your land troops."

It took Vico a moment to do the math – fifty dogs and cats at his command.

"Your air troops are not finalized yet," she continued. "However, I believe it will be comprised of crows and hawks."

He closed his eyes for a moment and withdrew his hand. The dog whuffed out a breath, but didn't move. He shifted slightly in order to touch the cat's still outstretched paw. He couldn't feel the texture of its pads, only its warmth. The cat blinked back at him.

"No fish?" he said, one side of his mouth twisting up.

"We have been unable to successfully implant cybernetics into aquatic subjects," Miranda answered. "But research is still ongoing."

"I was joking," Vico snapped, looking over his shoulder at her.

She looked back at him. "I know," she said simply. She looked back at her tablet and turned, walking towards the doors. "I'll escort you to your new quarters."

He lowered his arm and followed, refusing to look behind him. "They'd better be nicer than the old ones," he grumbled.

Life is not a fairy tale, nor is it a legend that gets embellished with every new telling, old men and women gesturing to wide-eyed babes. Life is something you survive or you don't: easy as that. Life is something you go through alone, and on rare occasions it meets up with someone else's and you can walk it together. At least until something comes along and makes it all explode in your face.

He knows, objectively, that it is not his fault that he had to leave his beautiful home as a child – that *war*, a word that explains both everything and nothing, was the reason they had to leave. But he also knows that it was his fault that he had to leave the one he carved out with his bare hands until dirt stained the edges of his fingernails, and his knuckles were raw with blood and sweat and effort. He knows that he failed them; that he flew them straight into hell and that when he crashed, they all did too. He knows he dragged them through Purgatory, and he hopes that they found something better than he did on the other side.

(There is a part of him that is terrified of being in command again; because if he couldn't save a group of professional soldiers, how the hell is he supposed to protect a slew of unwanted, untrained animals?)

The dog turned out to be a girl – he called her Moxie.

The cat was male – he called it Nero.

They never left his side, and they brought at least three other mammals with them at any given time. Moxie walked at his side, nudging at his new hand with her head when he fell still. Nero sat on his left shoulder, glaring at all that dared to look at him.

He had names for the other animals – he was up to nineteen dogs and thirteen cats, with more coming every few days – but they didn't sleep in his bed with him. Instead, the dogs slept against the walls of his quarters, curled up on blankets or cushions, with the cats claiming the long shelves that lined the walls, standing about four feet above the ground.

When Vico said, "Bed," they all went; when he named them, they answered. When they listened, his heart throbbed to the same pulse that his hand still flashed.

Then they gave him his ship.

It was… not what he was expecting.

"This is a passenger ship!" he snapped. On his right, Moxie was taunt and tense; on his shoulder, Nero was licking his front paw. "You gave me an airplane!"

Liu rolled his eyes and shoved his hands deeper in his pockets. It ruined the line of his uniform, but he wasn't the kind of person to care about those kinds of details. "Is that a problem?"

Miranda walked between them, her shoes clipping against the cement. Vico's newest addition, a falcon he had named Hermes, squawked a sharp cry at her, flying towards her.

"Hermes, return!" Vico snapped, holding out his left arm. The bird made a point of sweeping over Miranda's head as he turned (not that Miranda altered in her trajectory whatsoever), but came back, landing on Vico's wrist even as he continued arguing with Liu: "I was a pilot of a weaponized aircraft; this thing is useless to me!"

Liu frowned. "But, Baggio, you forget: you'll be carrying passengers."

All three animals looked at Liu; behind Vico, another dog huffed out a breath.

Vico clenched his teeth and his mechanical hand. "I am of more worth than a cargo pilot."

Liu exhaled a long breath. "Baggio, you haven't even checked it out. Why don't you use your eyes instead of your mouth for once?"

Nero hissed. Vico turned on his heel and snapped, "Hermes, scout!" The falcon lifted off his wrist and glided towards the plane. Vico followed, snapping his flesh fingers once to call the two dogs.

The first thing he noticed was that there was no cargo hold: although the plane was long – likely three hundred feet – and fairly wide – maybe fifty feet – it was only about fifteen feet high. And that was standing on its wheels.

The second thing he noticed was the window – one single pane of glass that stretched about one hundred feet. The other side was identical.

The third thing was that there were no seats inside. Instead, it was designed a lot like his quarters: each side with a wide shelf about four feet above the floor, and a series of hanging cages – all open – stretching across the ceiling. At the very front of the aircraft was a pilot's cabin: one chair, a huge panel, and a curved glass window.

He looked over his shoulder and said, "Explore!" Nero hopped off his shoulder and two other cats mysteriously appeared, trotting the length of one of the shelves. Moxie went straight for the pilot's· cabin, while the other dog, Hyde, sniffed out the floor. Hermes went straight into one cage and cried out again. The cage shook slightly with his weight; his talons were completely mechanical, as was his beak and the inside of his wings (supposedly).

Vico followed Moxie into the cabin and sat in the chair. He looked over the panel and focused on a small cluster of buttons.

"The cabin separates," he said.

"Yes," Miranda said behind him. He didn't flinch, but it was a near thing. "A hover unit."

He spun the chair around to face her where she stood in the open doorway between the cabin and the rest of the craft. "That's not very fuel efficient," he answered.

"Precisely 53% of this ship is constructed out of solar panels," she said. "There is a gasoline backup system for emergencies, however."

He rolled his eyes and spun the chair back around. "I

was teasing, Miranda."

"I would appreciate it if you refrained from flirting with me, Mr. Baggio," she replied.

He peered over the panel and patted Moxie on the head when she settled at his side. "Yeah, well, you're basically the only girl who talks to me; so what's a guy to do?"

"Refrain himself," she said, her voice dry. "On another note, we should have your fourth troop's beginning formation by the end of the week."

Moxie's tail thumped against the floor. Vico said, "New friends. Oh boy."

Satin was a very quiet crow. She was brilliant and vicious and came with fifteen others.

Vico spent half of his free time playing mediator between the four troops. It wasn't too different from his army days, though, so he didn't mind. He just created new whistles, snaps of fingers, and sounds all of them could distinguish.

They trained a *lot*. He made different orders for different tasks, and learned that one-word orders worked best. They found out what each troop excelled at, and that there were divisions of tasks within each troop.

His room began to smell like animal fur, and he got accustomed to a large black cat sitting on his chest most nights. He wore a leather armband on his left arm for the birds to land on and take off from, and a black, leather vest for the cats to hold onto when they sat on his shoulders. He kept a couple of dog treats in his back pocket for a job well done.

Baggio the Shepard, a few of the young soldiers and interns called him; he swore at them and sent a bird flying at them with talons outstretched.

Once upon a time, he used to speak fairly good French. Seemed that hell had taken that skill from him too.

He sat outside a small café at a round table with a croissant and a coffee in front of him and Moxie at his feet. Three tables down, another dog, Juniper, was mooching off an elderly couple for their scraps. On the top of the next table's parasol, one of his crows peered around, eyes black and glossy.

Moxie put a paw on his foot and he lifted it in response, using his heel as a fulcrum. "Non, mon ami," he muttered. "Pas maintenant." She huffed, but moved her paw off.

Then came the crash.

Vico had heard a lot of crashes in his lifetime: aircraft, sea vehicles, bicycles, hovercrafts, and automobile; but he still flinched at the sound of metal crunching and brakes squealing. He wondered what kind of vehicle it was – hover or electrical, large or small – and made sure to reach down and touch his flesh hand against Moxie's nose. Around him, people were exclaiming in French and rising to their feet. Juniper looked over to him, and he gave a single shake of his head.

(She was only eighteen months, poor thing. Still full of beans and eager to please.)

"Une ambulance! Quelqu'un appele une ambulance!"

"Alright," he murmured. "Time to go." He stood up,

snapped his metal fingers inside his coat pocket, and started walking, following the too-curious people that were headed towards the collision. If he looked up, he knew he'd see a crowd of birds, so he kept his eyes facing forward until he reached the site of the commotion.

It was a vehicle, small and electric and smashed into a light pole. There was a crowd of people swarming the car, and a couple of similar cars pulled up on the side-walk nearby. Across the street, a small Persian sat licking its front paw. It glanced over at Vico, and then stood, running off into an alley behind it. Vico kept walking; he refused to loiter or glance around to check on his troops. Instead, he kept his eyes forward, even when he heard the soft hum of hovercraft ambulances.

Liu looked over the report, finger tapping on the screen, and nodded to himself. "One pedestrian, and both the driver and the passenger injured; police and two ambulances tied up for an hour, leaving ample room for our primary force to secure the cargo." He glanced over at Vico with just his eyes. "And all because a cat ran across the road."

Vico stayed at-ease. He'd have to give Starshine an extra treat today.

Liu slide his finger down, shutting the tablet off. "Well, at least we know that works. On to Phase II."

If Vico were an introspective man, he wouldn't be in the position he currently found himself in. There would also have been a long period of time where he mused about the new arm and what it might mean to him later in life… But Vico wasn't an introspective man; it said so on his psych analysis.

(In case anyone was wondering, the arm was an incredible piece of machinery, and might have even been aesthetically pleasing had Vico consented to the skin graft. As it was, it was a silver skeleton, with transparent pieces visually exposing the wires (blue, red, and black) underneath while keeping everything neatly together. The joints were created with small spheres that flashed with softly pulsing light, to the same beat as his heart. It looked flimsy and fragile, but it was stronger than steel.

It would mean a lot to him later in life.)

Phase II was not well received by Vico.

"You killed my birds!" he shouted, storming into Liu's office.

Miranda glanced up and with a quick scan, tossed a small sphere onto the floor. It rolled to a stop between Vico and the desk, and created a barrier reaching from floor to ceiling and spreading about six feet across. It fizzled with electricity.

Liu raised his eyebrows. "What are you talking about, Baggio?" he asked.

"Operation Icarus," Miranda answered, already consulting her tablet. "It was a clue, Mr. Baggio." And she almost sounded kind, with the quick glance she darted his way.

Vico clenched his hands and wished he hadn't left his

troops at the Infirmary; wished he could click his tongue and send a cat with outstretched claws straight for their eyes. Because she was right, dammit, she was right; he should have known, should have made the connection. But he hadn't anticipated four of his crows – Lillian, Jack, Frost, and Bimbo – to spontaneously burst into flames like hellish phoenixes as they flew through the hospital's windows. He hadn't expected kamikaze crows.

Liu looked at him and folded his hands on his desk. "Let me get this straight, Baggio: You're not upset that we set a hospital on fire, resulting in the causalities of eighty-nine civilians, but that we used your troops to start it."

"They're my birds," he gritted out.

Liu's eyes narrowed. "They're *my* birds, Baggio. Just like you're my soldier. And whatever I order you to do, you'll do; understand?"

"No!" Vico snapped, kicking the small sphere. It sent a shock through his body and a ripple through the barrier. It made his breath catch in his chest, and he gritted his teeth. "Why bother making these birds if you're just gonna blow them up?"

"Why do people make bullets; why do people create bombs?" Liu retorted, getting to his feet in one smooth motion. "To serve a purpose; and if the weapon malfunctions, then we will dispose of it. Do you understand *that*, Baggio?"

Vico swore once, kicked the sphere again, and limped out of the office.

There were three squads of cybernetic animals. Vico's Wolf Pack, as he called them, was the largest and most varied, but also the newest. They trained every day, and because of their size, roamed the entire base, often scaring the new recruits by running between their legs.

Isabelle Mason had named her squad the City Spies. It was comprised of twenty-five rats and fifty pigeons. They were used for surveillance mostly, and stayed in designated areas of the base. For some reason, not everyone liked rats slinking across the walls or pigeons cooing in their ear while they tried to eat their lunch.

Rudy Anderson had The Hounds – ten Dobermans as vicious and strong as tigers. They returned from missions with blood-soaked muzzles and white scars on their torsos. They didn't answer to anyone but Anderson, and always travelled as a complete unit.

On the whole, Vico, Mason, and Anderson stayed on their own, choosing the company of their squads over that of any human. They were not friends in the least, and only tolerated the presence of the other two. Vico's cats liked to hunt Mason's rats, and Anderson's dogs growled at Vico's if they came too close.

The squad was loyal to the squad. They didn't need anyone else, and they didn't like anyone else either.

His troops began coming with collars. The birds wore bracelets on their ankles, and the dogs and cats shook and scratched at the new additions around their necks. Vico was given the colour code, and started a new diet of bitter guilt and rage.

Red collars meant that they were kamikaze fighters – this suicide portion comprised half of his crows and five of his smaller hawks. Within a few weeks, a rotation developed where he lost at least ten birds a mission. While he knew he shouldn't bother naming them, he had a routine down now; and how do you discriminate against creatures when they hadn't done anything wrong? They were like children: innocent, eager to please, and often incredibly stupid.

Vico had broken a lot of lives in his time; maybe this was karma slowly breaking his heart.

Then Marshmallow, a fluffy white cat, came back to him with a yellow collar. While Vico knew, according to the colour code, that this meant she was a conductor of some sort, it wasn't until they had a mission where they were supposed to fry the databanks of a company that he understood what it meant.

Unlike the kamikaze birds, where there was nothing left but a pile of ash and frayed wires, Vico was forced to collect the carcass of Marshmallow. The hot, dark smell of burnt hair stayed in his nose for hours, and lingered in his clothes.

"We haven't yet successfully calculated the amount of electricity a body can hold," Miranda said, fingers tapping at the screen in front of her. Vico's hair was still damp from the three showers he had taken to get the smell off his hands. "Too much cybernetic material and the subject loses its nature that makes it so useful as a weapon. Too little, and the body burns from excess of electricity." She swiped a finger to the right, and when the screen blinked black for a moment, Vico could see her reflection. Her lips were curled up at the corners. "It's a fascinating experiment," she said.

Something curdled in his stomach.

Black collars were spies – with cybernetic eyes and cameras installed inside. When he got that notice, he stroked a hand down Nero's back and said, "Does that make you a spy too? I remember that eye of yours."

Nero opened one eye – his real one – sent Vico a dirty look, and then closed it again. A few seconds later, he began to purr.

There were other collars, other jobs, other things that broke his heart, but Vico tried not to think about it. He compartmentalized. Soldiers died. It happened. It even happened under his control.

But somehow it was different when you fed the soldier by hand, and gave them an ear scratch, or cleaned them of their loose feathers, or brushed out their fur, and then sent them out to die.

Satin was pissed at him – but Vico didn't really blame her. Every week, she lost a portion of her troops, and Vico was the one ordering them. Still, she didn't have to peck his flesh hand every time he poured out her food; he was getting tired of walking down to Infirmary twice a day for disinfectant spray and a bandage.

He was walking back from one of those trips, rubbing at the bandage – the nurse was either new or grumpy, and hadn't wrapped it very tight, and it was lumpy and distracting and would be itchy in an hour – when he saw Miranda standing in a room by herself. This wasn't unusual, Miranda was about as social a creature as he was, but what was unusual was what was on the large screen she was standing before. It wasn't her usual charts and diagrams – it looked like maps and graphs.

He walked over to the door and opened it, stepping inside. He moved towards the screen and stopped at Miranda's left shoulder, taking in the information. It looked like some sort of shipping information, something coming from the States.

"Is there something you required?" Miranda asked, fingers tapping away at her personal tablet.

"That new nurse is terrible," he answered, eyes still scanning the screen.

"She doesn't approve of your personality," Miranda responded, eyes flicking down to her screen. "I do hope you're not suggesting we fire her."

"And why not?" Vico countered, rubbing at his hand again. The texture was weird under the robotic finger.

"If we fired everyone who disapproved of your personality, operations at this base would grind to a halt." She reached out to tap a finger on the large screen – it changed to a grid of the east coast of the States. "You don't have clearance to view this material."

"You're sure going out of your way to keep me from seeing this too," he said. "What's all this about anyways?"

"A new shipment," she responded. "This is for our newest squad."

"Another squad?"

"Domestic animals," she said, eyes flicking back and forth between the tablet and the screen. "Goats, pigs, sheep… We're hoping to move into another area." She tapped on the screen again. "However, this requires new equipment; each species has certain requirements, with a different criteria for effectiveness-"

"You're kinda sadistic, Miranda," he interrupted.

She paused, actually stopping mid-sentence. "I beg your pardon?" she questioned the screen, finger barely touching it.

"You love this," Vico said, no emotion in his voice. "You are taking animals, destroying their lives and the lives of innocent people, and all you can focus on is how to make them more effective, while keeping them as alive as possible."

She brought her finger to her chin, and slowly rotated on her heel to face him. "Mr. Baggio, sadism is defined as deriving sexual pleasure from inflicting pain on another individual," she said. "I am not inflicting pain for the sake of my own gratification; I am experimenting and working on a final solution of biological and cybernetic co-existence. If specimens are injured or killed in the process, that is merely a fact." She raised an eyebrow. "Pretending to care for something beyond the finished project seems like an excessive waste of energy to me."

Vico watched her face for an expression. "You're very cold, Miranda."

She rolled her eyes and turned back to the screen. "And your life is a clear testament that being passionate is an admirably characteristic." He clenched his metal fist, and exhaled slowly through his nose. She watched this reaction from the corner of her eye before adding, "Terran Engineering allows me to explore my research. They fund it without placing limitations on my work. What more could a girl ask for?"

Vico scowled, and said, "Yeah, well, explain that to my dead troops." Then he stormed out of the room.

And sometimes, when Nero felt the need to support his troop – usually while they were on the Ark, as Vico had taken to calling his aircraft – a huge orange and white cat named Fat Ass would hop up onto Vico's bed, and stretch out on his chest. Vico didn't really like not being able to breathe, so he'd give Fat Ass a swat, but Fat Ass seemed to take it as a sign of love, because he'd just roll over on his back.

The birds whispered above his head, chittering at each other, and grooming their feathers. There were a couple of soft thuds as a couple of dogs pawed at each other, trying to get comfortable. Moxie rested her head on Vico's leg, and huffed out a cloud of hot breath.

Vico stared at the ceiling, and used his metal hand to scratch at Fat Ass' stomach. He pawed at the metal, squirming until he fit a metal finger in his mouth. Then he began to chew on it. Vico sighed.

Miranda was correct about one thing: the metal forearm and hand was recognizable, and it did draw attention. People tended to stare at it, and then at Vico, with their eyes finally falling on whatever animal was hanging around him at the time. They avoided him; called him a robot, called him hotheaded, called him an animal, and didn't care about the contradictions of these names.

And Vico found himself looking in the mirror some

days, and being unable to recognize the man he used to be. He kept himself clean-shaven still, mostly because the crows like to pull out his hair, and the dogs sometimes drooled on his face when they got too excited. But his hair was getting shaggy, and his clothes were no longer neat, and his smile was difficult to find now. He was used to the softly flashing lights of his hand, and accustomed to the way light reflected off his forearm, but sometimes reached out expecting to feel softness or coarseness, and instead only registering the heat of the object.

Once upon a time, he was Major Ludovico Baggio; for a while, he was simply Bags. Now he was Vico Baggio, with a leather vest, dog drool on his pants, and cat hair on his shirt. He scowled and grunted, snapped fingers and stomped feet. The only women who spoke to him were the nurses or Miranda, and the only men were the ones who gave him orders. He practiced shooting five hours a week, and snuck into the Weaponry on the third level, poking around without asking permission.

For all that he had a metal arm, he stuck close to the basics: his animals, his favourite outfit, and a couple of six-inch knifes and a semi-automatic handgun. They tried to make him use the handheld machine guns, the laser guns, the immobilizing pistols, and he refused. He liked the classics too much. But he loved the soft zoom of The Ark, the 3D screen for missions, and the hovering ability of the pilot's cabin. He got a hold of a hovercycle, and took the dogs for runs, and the birds for flights; shooting across fields at 60mph, with the dogs running easily at his side, and the birds doing lazy loops in the sky, waiting for a challenge.

The cats, well... Cats would do whatever the hell they wanted; best to leave them to it.

Apparently, the shipment that Miranda was so fascinated in was due to arrive tomorrow. Not that it affected Vico in any way, since him and his troops were being sent out to the Netherlands to cause an Air-Dock incident.

Vico stood in the doorway separating his pilot's cabin from the rest of the Ark, watching his animals settle in for the ride. He glanced down at Moxie, sitting at his side, and said, "Whadd'ya say, girl? Second star to the right, straight on 'til morning?"

She looked back up at him, and thumped her tail against the floor. Hermes let out a loud cry, and Satin pulled on his hair, plucking a handful right out of his scalp. When he turned to look into his cabin, Nero was sitting in his chair, grooming his genitals again.

"Dammed cat," Vico grumbled, stepping over. He swatted Nero up the side of his head, and hustled him out of his chair. When Nero removed himself, after hissing at Vico, Vico took his seat, and started pulling lever and pushing buttons.

First, he activated the solar panels, bringing energy to the engines; then he fired up the thrusters, following with the propellers in the back. Beneath them, the Ark began to hum, and the animals began to whine, and cry.

Moxie let out a single bark, while Hermes and Satin cried out in unison. Nero hopped up onto a shelf, and flicked his tail once.

The Ark fell silent.

Vico mentally reviewed the mission parameters, considered the three crows he was going to lose, the two cats and one dog that was supposed to ruin the computer system of the Air Control, and the five spy-hawks that were supposed to report back. He knew Liu and Miranda didn't understand why he had to bring all his troops for a simple eleven-man mission; but he didn't have to explain much to them. As long as the job got done…

He cracked the knuckles of his flesh hand, and wiggled the metal fingers. He said, turning his head to look down at Moxie, "One day, we won't have to answer to anyone. What do you think about that?"

And Moxie whined.

Melanie Collins

The incredibly funny and talented Melanie Collins seems to excel in all the diverse things she does. Melanie is an avid lover of science fiction, fantasy, cosplay, and gaming; and in 2005, co-founded Sci-Fi on the Rock.

In 2010, this down-to-Earth pet groomer added author to her list of credits when "Woven by the Thief" appeared to critical acclaim in the original *Sci-Fi from the Rock* anthology. Since then, Melanie has continued trailblazing along the path of cool girl geekdom, kicking butt with 8 Limb Muay Thai in St. John's, and doing some serious good for charity with local non-profit Sandbox Gaming.

"Woven by the Thief" appears here in print again as a testament to her many talents.

Woven by the Thief

A soft breath escaped her in the barely morning hours, the thick sheets twisted tightly around her body as she shifted again and turned atop the mattress. The chill of the late fall's damp night easily penetrated the small home's walls and its effect was noted in the sleeping woman's posture, but not in her expression.

He found her fascinating, through and through. The way she escaped to a world where she was warm, comforted, and happy, when the truth of her surroundings were more than enough to oppress the happiness of so many others... it captivated him. It had captivated him since she was a child, as he was, and when she had reached the time of her days where he would no longer be needed, he felt the sting of losing something so close that he had never understood, never been allowed to understand as they grew alongside each other.

It was chance, pure coincidence that he should find her again after so long. Nearly a decade apart, and yet he knew instantaneously as he stumbled across her sleeping form that it was her. It must be her. Every night he could find the reason to do so, he left from his appointed task long enough to steal a glimpse at her. Trapped, like he was, she could still escape to dreams dreams he did not even have to weave. Glancing to the large and finely woven pouch beside him to ensure its package was still intact, his mind was set at ease for the great violation of his privileges he had come to commit on a startlingly regular basis now.

The air of the room just beyond the windowsill was so drastically warmer that it was like it enveloped his tiny, fragile frame in a familiar embrace, his wings flitting silently through the dark. Whispers in the stagnant night flowed softly from his lips, the melodic sing song he had been taught as a memory tool, and the glowing lights that swirled with them as they fell from him toward the floor like drifting petals grew in their bright sparkling as more joined. His arm extended like another wing as he took a swooping turn in flight, the sparks colliding with one another to bathe the entire room in a soft, blue haze before it broke as it always did, the silence destroyed by beauty and magnificence.

The symphony echoed about the room, its harmonies and intricacies all a delicious serving for him and only him to enjoy outside of the realm of her mind. Tonight it was soft, sweet, and romantic, but with such a suspenseful and mysterious undertone that it drove him all the deeper into curiosity. His eyes closed as he hovered directly above her, deep inhalations filling him with every essence of the masterpiece that emanated from her.

The stories of old would label him a "tooth fairy," when in truth there were never any teeth taken. Not long into his years of life did he cease the childish pondering as to why a tooth taker is seen in a much more positive light than a dream harvester; why they would look down on him for what he did, but not what they would've claimed he did. Yet none of that bothered him now, none of it reached his thoughts as he bathed in the pure eloquence of a fully embraced fantasy beyond the eyelids of the woman beneath him. A taste much too rich to harvest, something so defined and ripe that it erupted into the purest of art forms he knew: to take this perfect piece away from its conductor would be to rip the soul, and the damage sustained through years of awaking too early kills enough dreams without his hand to aid it.

Children need to learn that dreams are dreams; they are not real. They cannot be real. Children are taught through the weaving and taking that they must focus all of their heart upon the reality around them and not the reality their eyelids are painted with beyond the end of the day. Through that, can it be assumed that dreams are more precious when you've grown? That the escape from the cold reality of a chilled room in a damp and dreary world is more appreciated, understood?

Could it be that it becomes vital for the survival of love, creativity, and passion?

The orchestrated illusion echoed about him in its twisting and turning, the soft and soothing tranquillity of a moment frightfully changing at times to a jump and dash... dreams are not planned. Dreams are not set in stone. Every movement of your eyes, every thump of your heartbeat, every breath, every flinch, every slight movement of the muscles upon your sleeping form create notes, harmonies   they set the tempo of the symphony that your soul plays with more emotion than one can possibly know how to feel.

The small eyes on his small body opened once again as he gazed down toward the sleeping woman beneath him. Fingers sprawled outward above her as more whispering accompanied the sounds about him, swirls of purple and green mist illuminating the room in a soft glow extended their way from him to her, a window into her dream drawing back its curtains to allow his sensations to peer inside fully. The world of her dream opened before him in splendid fashion, as it had so often these past nights when he had stolen away into her home against the laws of his kind, and basked in someone else's escape from reality.

The mist of colour surrounding him like a translucent cocoon seemed to lower him slowly in a haze of bliss to land just beside her dormant form encased within the taut wrapped sheets and he fell backwards, sitting with a cushioned 'thud' upon the plush pillow while he watched her adventure unfold. Would adult's dreams still conduct themselves in the surreal way they do, were they not conditioned to see it as the norm when young? Would such a real, loving moment unfolding in a dream be so prone to interruption by an unbelievable, unacceptable cameo of something so disenchanting if children were not to learn that dreams and reality must be forever kept apart?

His heart, however much of one a 'dream thief' can claim to have, ached as it always did at the questions which continued to replay themselves for yet another night in his own escape from his own reality: What would her dream sound like, if he had not been the one to scar her soul so many times as she grew? Would the masterpiece he heard flow with the emotions of a full and uninterrupted story? Would she, or anyone, still receive those moments in so many lonely night escapes where a good dream can turn so sour and frightening in the blink of an eye, or where a moment of painful and agonizing real emotion can be whisked away by the most blunt of reminders that it 'must be a dream'?

A shift; her coiled form stretching and rolling before him as he drew himself out of his own thoughts just enough to observe. Her eyes opened in the dark room, the shine from what little light available permeating the haze of the green and purple that marked his hands as weaving thoughts and fantasies and dreams and imaginings that did not belong to him. They drifted to him sleepily, her mind not nearly awake, and he saw himself flash within her dream: his form so perfectly displayed as though a photograph was taken   though he felt this image somehow looked younger.

Another shift; this time within the expression upon on her face as unconsciously, yet with more conscious emotion and thought than one can possibly know how to experience, she smiled a look of true appreciation toward him as the image reflected his age   the age which he and her shared. Then, in his moments of doubt and worry and depression, did he feel forgiven for what he criticized himself so harshly for. You cannot leave someone to neglect the difference between reality and dreams, for in dreams you hold the ability to choose more destiny than you can reach in the real world. You need a place you can escape to, where you can feel so in control while everything is so out of control.

Collecting the woven bag of dream seeds from the sill as he left again into the frosted night air, he reflected that it was alright to make the heart breaking decision to leave his image so clear, precise and solid within her thoughts and memories that night. That it would be alright if someone, somewhere, remembered him for what he was; for whom he was.

Because, after all, who would think it to be anything more than a dream?

Peter J. Foote

Born and raised in the Annapolis Valley of Nova Scotia, the son of an apple farmer, Peter Foote studied archaeology in university, is employed as a boiler and refrigeration operator, and runs a used bookstore out of his basement in his spare time.

Believing that an author should write what he knows, many of Peter's stories are a reflection of his personal life.

"The Silence Between Moons" is Peter's first published story.

The Silence Between Moons

Pressing his fingers into the muddy footprint and bringing them to his nose, the ranger flinches away. *Goblins. Close from the smell of it.* Using the light from the rising full moon, the ranger surveys the area carefully before notching an arrow in his bow and silently melding into the undergrowth of the forest.

Dancing between the shafts of moonlight that spear their way through the naked tree branches, the ranger follows the path that the goblins have made easily, almost too easily, as if they were making no secret of their passing. Fearing a trap, the ranger slows his rush, squats down on his heels, and scans his surroundings carefully, his nose in the air and the notched arrow in his bow like an eye stabbing into the darkness.

Sensing nothing, the ranger rises, and in doing so, sees the moonlight highlight more tracks, those of wolves and the distinctive outline of a naked human foot. Shocked that a human would be out here alone, and clearly not wearing boots, the ranger is filled with dread, an emotion magnified seconds later as a mournful wolf's cry echoes through the trees. Leaving all semblance of stealth behind, the ranger crashes through the undergrowth, the branches whipping his face and brambles digging and clawing at his clothes as if they were purposely trying to slow him.

Before long, the sounds of battle reach his ears: the guttural language of the goblins, the snap of powerful jaws closing on flesh, and the cry of a human voice. Pushing back the waves of exhaustion that threaten to overwhelm him, the ranger bursts through a last tangle of dead blackberry canes and comes upon a battle.

With the moonlight shining behind the ranger, it could almost be a scene from a play. A woman, petite, dark and beautiful stands naked before a group of goblins, swinging a tree branch protectively over a dead wolf at her feet with a goblin spear through its body.

Rooted in place taking in the scene, the ranger can only watch as one of the goblins gets past the woman's defenses and hits her in the left temple with its club. The ranger can only watch in horror as the woman falls upon the dead wolf at her feet, before he curses his inactivity, lets out a cry of rage and draws his bow. His cry startles the goblins just as they start to reach for their prize, while the goblin with the war club is startled by the sudden appearance of an arrowhead jutting from its throat before it collapses into a bloody heap.

Tossing aside his bow, the ranger draws a pair of hand axes from his belt and rushes towards the goblins. Turning to meet this assault, the three remaining goblins recover and fan out in an effort to flank the ranger. Though outnumbered three to one, the ranger nevertheless takes the battle to the goblins, and with a quick feint is able draw one armed with a rusty dagger into making a wild slash.

The ranger easily blocks this clumsy attack with crossed hand-axes before countering with a kick to the creature's gut, and when the goblin doubles over in pain, sinks one of his narrow hand-axes into its spine.

Here the ranger's luck runs out, for when he tries to pull his hand-axe from the back of the goblin that lays twitching at his feet, he finds that it's stuck in the spine of the creature. Sensing that they now have the upper hand, the remaining two goblins advance on the ranger. One, presumably the leader with its numerous scars, leather breastplate, and serrated short sword, gives a broken tooth grin at its fellow and lunges at the ranger's belly with its wicked blade. Abandoning the stuck hand-axe, the ranger tries to turn away from the oncoming blade, but is only partly successful as the serrated blade rips through the ranger's tunic and leaves a ragged line of crimson along his ribcage. Gasping in pain, the ranger instinctively clasps his free hand over the wound on his side and with his remaining hand-axe held out protectively in front of him, prepares for the next attack.

The last goblin seems happy to let its leader have all the fun as it waves its meat cleaver in the air and cheers loudly. Basking in its underling's praise, the goblin leader fails to see the change in the ranger's body language as he slowly grinds the balls of his feet into the soft ground. With the wicked sword held up, the goblin leader lets out a roar and rushes the wounded ranger. A puzzled look quickly flashes across the creature's ugly face as it tries to understand what it is seeing. Instead of a defeated human ready to be put to slaughter, a feral grin crosses the ranger's lips as he leaps up to meet the goblin's rush with one of his own, catching the goblin in the chest with his head and causing the pair of them to collapse in a tangled heap.

The goblin leader is the first to recover, and it grasps its sword handle with both hands to bring it down upon the ranger's shoulder, which causes him to drop his hand-axe from nerveless fingers. Dizzy from his wounds, the ranger uses his body weight to hold down the goblin as his hands try madly to find the creature's throat. The bug-eyed face of the goblin leader, quickly turning blue in the moonlight, is suddenly thrown into harsh shadow. Seeing it, the ranger releases his grip and rolls away just as the last goblin is completing the downward swing with its heavy meat cleaver. Unable to stop its momentum, the goblin can only watch in horror as the cleaver sinks itself into the leader's throat, causing a fountain of blood to escape and splatter.

The look of horror on the goblin's face is intensified as the ranger sits up, his face awash in goblin blood, white teeth gleaming in the moonlight. Screaming in terror, the last goblin flees into the night, the sounds of its passage a stark contrast to the quiet of the scene of battle.

Rising upon shaky legs, the ranger rubs his numb shoulder as he gathers up his weapons, the hand-axe in the back of the goblin making a sickening sound as it is pulled free, before going to check on the woman.

In other circumstances it could have been a lovely scene, a naked woman lying atop a wolf pelt surrounded in moonlight like the marble pillars of a temple. Instead, the woman is plastered in mud and bleeding from a nasty scalp wound, the wolf dead from a goblin spear and the moonlight signaling that frost is in the air.

While her skin is cold to the touch, her pulse is strong, and the ranger lets out a breath he has been unconsciously holding. Tearing off a piece of his slashed tunic, the ranger fashions a hasty bandage around her scalp, wraps her in his cloak, and slings the woman over his shoulder, letting out a gasp of pain as the wound on his side flares in pain.

Just as the ranger is about to turn away, he looks down at the dead wolf that apparently died to protect the woman and wonders at the connection between the two. It's a small enough courtesy, but he pulls free the jagged goblin spear and tosses it into the woods before resetting the burden on his shoulder.

Dawn is breaking and the last of the full moon fades away as a monstrous looking figure walks out of the woods. Hunchbacked, its feet drag across the frost covered ground leaving a path a drunken sailor would envy, and its steam-laden breath trails behind like a magical cloak.

Pausing briefly to catch his breath and once again adjust the weight of the wounded woman, the ranger takes in a deep lungful of crisp autumn air and looks upon his home. Built with his own two hands, the simple one room cabin might not be much to look at with its moss covered roof and single window, but the walls are tight and the stone chimney sound, and it is his haven from the monster called civilization.

Berating himself for wool-gathering when safety and warmth are just a stone's throw away, the ranger checks to make sure the woman is still breathing easily and goes home.

With the last of his energy the ranger pushes aside the scattering of books atop his cot before gently placing the woman on his bed and covering her with his thickest bear-skin. For several moments he stares down at the woman, taking in her suntanned skin, calloused feet and rough fingernails, her beauty still clear under it all. Shaking himself out of his daze, the ranger leaves the bedside and gathers up sticks and tinder to kindle a fire in the stone fireplace. Sliding down the peeled log wall, the ranger kicks off his mud encrusted boots, puts his feet near the fire and mutters, "I really should put some water on to boil..." and promptly falls into an exhausted slumber.

Daylight streaming in the cabin's single window slowly creeps across the split log floor, the dust dancing in the column of light as it makes its way across the ranger's chest before finally resting on his face. Groaning in discomfort, the ranger turns his face away from the brightness and by doing so wakes himself up. "Augh, my head," he mutters as he cradles his head in his hands, and seeing them covered in blood brings the night's activities crashing home.

Looking up from his place on the floor, the ranger looks to his bed to see the woman from the night before crouched in the corner staring wild-eyed at him, wrapped in the bear skin and faintly panting.

Forcing lightness in his voice, the ranger says, "How are we doing now? I don't know about you, but I'm pretty stiff and sore;" and with cautious movements slowly stands, all the while watching the woman from the corner of his eye. "Are you in pain? Can I check your head?"

The woman rears back in the bed when the ranger tries to step towards her.

"Okay, maybe in a bit. Why don't I get the fire started and make us some tea, would you like that?" Silence being his only response, the ranger turns his back to the woman and busies himself trying to rekindle the fire from a few glowing coals all the while humming softly. Careful not to make any sudden movements, the ranger builds up the fire and hangs a kettle of water over the growing flames.

Falling into his familiar kitchen routine, the ranger almost forgets the woman is there until she speaks. "Why do you have fire in your den? Is it because you have no pack mates to lay with and keep you warm?"

The ranger's hand freezes in mid-motion for a brief second before continuing the job of placing dried leaves and herbs in the kettle over the fire. "Den?" the ranger mutters under his breath as he turns back towards the woman only to find her sitting up in his bed, the bearskin pooled around her legs. Hastily averting his eyes away from her nakedness, the ranger replies in a shaky voice, "I guess that's part of the reason I have a fire inside, to keep me warm at night. Don't you use a fire where you live?"

Silence.

Soon the small cabin is filled with the smell of dried herbs steeping in the kettle, a clean and purifying smell that is a sharp contrast to the rancid odor of sticky goblin blood that seems to hover over the ranger.

With his back to the woman, the ranger gently peels off his torn and bloody tunic, gasping in pain as the fabric is pulled away from the ragged cut in his side. Throwing the soiled tunic into the far corner, the ranger splashes the last of his fresh water in a chipped ceramic bowl and begins to clean the wound with a cloth.

He is startled when a small hand stops him and carefully removes the cloth from his hand. Frozen in place for fear of spooking her, the ranger watches as the woman gently washes his wound, very conscious of her nakedness so close to him, long dormant feelings bring a flush to his skin.

When she is done, the ranger inspects the wound and sees that it isn't as bad as he feared, a ragged cut but not deep and no sign of infection. Smiling in thanks, he slowly kneels down beside the woman and reaches up to remove the makeshift bandage from around her head. Her eyes go wide and she starts to draw back, so he stops and starts to hum an old lullaby that he remembers his mother singing to him when he was young. The look of fear slowly leaves her as the ranger gently unwinds the bandage, but he can feel the tenseness course through her body, like a drawn bow.

Still humming, the ranger carefully washes away the dried blood to inspect her head wound, but rocks back on his heels as he finds the wound gone without any trace of a scar. Instead, a shock of white hair is quickly growing in an otherwise sea of black, like moonlight against the night, the only sign that there had been a wound at all.

Giving the woman a weak smile once he is done, the

ranger helps her to rise and steers her towards the bed and fallen bearskin. Seeing her once again wrapped up, the ranger absently goes to the steeping kettle and pours two mugs of herbal tea, occasionally risking a quick glance at the strange woman and shaking his head in wonder.

Carrying over the two mugs of herbal tea, the ranger puts them on the floor in front of the woman and says, "We'll let these cool for a minute while I go get some more fresh water, and then we'll have a little talk, okay? Maybe start with your name? I'm called Peadar."

Pulling on a fresh tunic and jamming his feet into his boots, Peadar grabs his water bucket and leaves the cabin, making sure to pull the cabin door tightly shut. Squatting at the edge of the nearby stream, Peadar tips his bucket into the water, careful not to stir up any sediment. He looks back in the direction of the cabin.

"Clearly there's magic involved here, though how and what its nature is, I don't know. It's almost as if she's fae touched."

Peadar is almost back to his cabin before he realizes that something is wrong: the door stands wide open and the bearskin lays discarded on the ground. Dropping the water bucket, Peadar races towards his cabin despite knowing what he will find when he gets there. A cabin empty except for two steaming mugs of herbal tea.

Quickly donning his cloak, Peadar grabs his bow and quiver and hurries outside, frantically following the woman's footprints in the cold wet ground.

Hours later, just as the sun throws its final rays above

the treetops, Peadar stumbles out of the forest. Pale and haggard, shoulders slumped in defeat, the ranger stops outside his cabin, picks up the fallen bearskin when the woman dropped it all those hours ago. Bringing the bearskin up to his face, he closes his eyes and inhales deeply. With one last longing look behind him, Peadar turns away from the forest and enters his cabin.

Just as the waning moon starts its journey across the heavens, Peadar pounds the last of six stakes into the ground. Formed into a rough circle in front of his cabin, the ranger secures a torch to each and sets them alight. Satisfied that his beacons will stay lit, Peadar raises his face to the starry sky and mutters a faint pray before retreating to his cabin.

Tossing and turning in his narrow bunk, books scattered, bearskin kicked to the floor, and sheets twisted around his legs like the tentacles of a sea monster, Peadar moans in his sleep for several minutes before bolting upright and crying out.

"Dear God, what a nightmare! I can still hear the howling of the beast." Wiping sweat off his brow with a shaky hand, Peadar freezes in mid-motion before craning his neck towards the door of his cabin. "I can still hear the howling!" Jumping out of this cot, Peadar hastily pulls on his trousers, grabs his pair of hand axes, and rushes into the cold night.

Most of his torches are still alight, though bits of rag and pitch drip from them casting flickering shadows around him, almost like fairies dancing. With axes held ready, Peadar walks barefoot across the cold wet grass to the edge of the pool of light. Straining his ears for any trace of the sound that woke him, Peadar realizes that he doesn't hear anything at all, not the cry of an owl, or a squirrel in the undergrowth, not even the fall leaves rustling on their branches. It's almost as if the whole world is holding its breath.

On the edge of his vision motion catches his eye, but when he looks to its source, he sees nothing. Again it happens, but no matter how fast he turns, he can't get a clear look. Tired of being played with, Peadar takes a firmer grip on his hand axes, and slowly walks into the centre of the ring of torches.

Flickering torchlight dances across tense muscles and highlights the cloud of the ranger's breath as it meets the cold air, but still nothing happens. A test of wills is being played out but who will blink first?

First one pair of eyes can be seen shining in the torchlight, then another, and another, until nearly a dozen sets of yellow eyes stare out at the ranger. A low throaty growl starts which is quickly picked up by the rest, each voice an individual but coming together like a chorus, building in volume until the very trees seem to shrink back in fear.

Gripping his axes tighter, Peadar braces for the attack that he is sure is coming, and just when he can stand the growling no longer, it stops so suddenly that he is almost deafened by the silence.

Out of the darkness she walks, black as midnight, lean and powerful muscles rippling under her dark fur as she stalks back and forth at the edge of the torchlight before walking up to Peadar. Yellow eyes flickering with intelligence stare up at him, lock on and draw him deeper into their depths. Unconsciously, Peadar drops the axes as he leans towards the she-wolf, the area completely quiet except for the sputtering and hissing of the torches.

As quickly as it started, the connection between the two is broken as the she-wolf turns away from the ranger and walks back towards the darkness. Just at the edge of the pool of light she turns back and Peadar notices that her beautiful black coat isn't complete, for over her left brow is a shock of white hair like the moon in the night's sky.

In the clear light of the following day, Peadar tries to convince himself that the night before was all a dream brought on by goblin attack and his concern for the missing woman, until he sees the ground around his cabin littered with wolf tracks.

Unsure what it all means, Peadar decides to stay close to his cabin today and tend to the wood pile getting it ready for winter. Soon the clearing around the cabin echoes with the sounds of wood being chopped as Peadar, stripped down to his trousers, splits log after log. The comforting manual labour keeps his body busy while allowing his mind to retreat and reflect upon what he experienced last night.

As impossible as it seems, it's clear that the she-wolf and the woman are connected, probably one in the same, though how this is possible I don't understand. All the tales I've read suggest it's during the three days of the full moon that a person becomes a wolf creature, not the other way around. And she seems to be one or the other, not a twisted mixture of the two, nor did I get a feeling that she meant me harm, the opposite in fact.

Hours later finds Peader both physically and mentally exhausted as he lounges against his cot, book in his lap and lukewarm mug of herbal tea at his elbow. Squinting at the fine lettering in the flickering candlelight, Peadar finally decides to give up and call it a night. Banking the coals in the fireplace with an iron poker, Peadar's hand freezes in mid-motion as his ears perk up and he turns towards the door. Absently replacing the poker, Peadar goes to the door and lifts the latch with a shaky hand. The cold night air instantly invades the tiny cabin, robbing it of its stored warmth, but Peadar fails to notice as he walks outside.

"There it is again, I knew I heard something..." mutters Peadar in the darkness. The howl of a lone wolf echoes through the night, the call rising and falling in pitch and tone as it floats down from above. Eyes straining in the darkness, Peadar looks to the nearby rise and is just able to make out the silhouette of a wolf. Maybe the wolf senses Peadar or maybe it can see him highlighted by the light spilling out of the cabin door, but either way it stops and howls again. This time there can be no mistake; it is clearly a greeting, calling one soul to another. Heedless of the cold, Peadar smiles and raises a hand in silent salute to the wolf. The greeting acknowledged, the wolf turns away, and in doing so the waning moonlight highlights the tuft of white hair on the she-wolf's brow.

For the rest of the month, this ritual is repeated: just after sunset Peadar walks outside and awaits the she-wolf. Without fail she is on the rise every night to issue her greeting to the ranger, which he returns with a wave.

While she never comes closer than the rise during their nightly greetings, she makes her presence known in other ways. Several times throughout that first month the ranger wakes up to find a dead rabbit at his door, its neck broken, but unmarred on any other way.

A month later, just as the full moon rises in the night sky, Peadar dons his heavy cloak and prepares to go out for the nightly greeting. Opening the cabin door, he is startled to find the woman there, naked as she was the last time he saw her. In shock, Peadar just stands there woodenly as the woman slowly reaches out and snakes her hand through the buttons of his tunic to run her fingers lightly over the fresh scar from the goblin's blade. Keeping her hand against his side, she looks Peadar in the eyes and says, "My name is Shadow."

Something breaks within Peadar, as he lets out a great sigh and removes his cloak to gently wrap around Shadow before leading her inside the cabin, closing the door firmly behind them.

This cycle repeats all winter. Most nights Peadar and Shadow conduct their nightly ritual, she from the rise, he from outside his cabin; but for the three days and nights of the month when the moon is full, she comes to him in human form and they stay warm and comfortable within the tiny cabin as the snow falls and the wind blows.

Their time together is wild and carefree, without plan or thoughts to the future. The few times Peadar asks Shadow about her past and nature, she diverts him to the small cot and a sly smile. After a while, Peadar stops asking and decides that when she wants to tell him she will. Similarly, she doesn't seem to care about his life before they met nor even his days when they aren't together. For Shadow, the world seems broken up into two experiences: the time they are together and everything else.

Nothing lasts forever, not even winter.

Finally the days start getting longer, the snows starts to melt and nature begins her cycle of renewal. With spring there is also empty cupboards and foodstuffs that can't be gleamed off the land, so Peadar packs up his sled with the pelts he harvested through the winter and makes the long trip to the town.

Where before he saw dirty, unhappy people living on top of each other in an unending dim of noise and open sewers, Peadar's eyes start noticing other things. There, an old couple walking arm in arm as they navigate icy patches in the road, there, a young couple sneaking a kiss behind a hay wagon, and there a father carrying his son on his shoulders laughing and joking.

Peadar barely remembers the trip back to his little cabin as he replays the scenes he saw in the town over and over in his mind, but instead of the strangers he inserts Shadow and himself.

His mind made up, Peadar decides that tonight he will act. As the spring sun starts to dip below the trees, he leaves his cabin dressed for speed, only his canteen and hand axes to slow him down.

A happy grin is stamped on his face as he dashes through the forest steadily making his way higher, and before long Peadar breaks from the forest and arrives at the rise. Looking down at his cheery cabin, a tiny wisp of chimney smoke snaking itself to the heavens, Peadar finds himself filled with hope. Taking a pull from his canteen, Peadar squats down and waits.

His wait isn't long.

Out of the darkness she stalks, beautiful and deadly, her tuft of white hair in a sea of black flashing in the moon-light. Making sure to make no sudden movement, Peadar slowly rises and keeps his hands by his side.

"Hello Shadow, I thought I would greet you tonight," says Peadar in a soft low voice.

His years as a ranger weren't wasted since it's clear that the she-wolf didn't know Peadar was here until he spoke. With hackles raised and lips curled, the she-wolf paces around the ranger, first one way then another, her nose high in the air capturing his scent. As suddenly as it started, it stops as the she-wolf relaxes and gives Peadar's hand a tiny lick before leaning against his legs.

Running his hands through her midnight coat, Peadar tries to give voice to the day's experiences. "I thought we could spend more time together during the rest of the month, maybe I could even run with you and the pack sometime, maybe tonight?"

The attack was so sudden that Peadar has no idea what is happening until he finds himself on the cold hard ground and Shadow is standing on his chest, her nails digging though his tunic and her snarling fangs hovering above his face.

Staring into the yellow eyes of Shadow, the look of bewilderment on Peadar's face is slowly replaced by the dawning of understanding as the blood drains from his face and his eyes moist over. Her message hitting its mark, the she-wolf steps back allowing Peadar to sit up.

The two stare at each other for a few heartbeats, until Shadow turns away and without a backward glance melts into the night. Where a short time ago he had a spring in his step, now Peadar moves like an old man, as he gathers up his belongings and shuffles home, wiping his eyes on his tunic sleeve.

For the rest on the month, Peadar goes about his normal routine listlessly, wandering about with shoulders slumped and head bowed. At night he remains inside his cabin reading, pointedly ignoring the solitary wolf cry that echoes on the wind.

"Steady man, get control of yourself," Peadar mutters to himself as he paces back and forth within his tiny cabin, each trip casting a quick glance out the window at the darkening sky. "You're going to make yourself sick if you continue acting this way, maybe it will work out." Reaching for his cup of herbal tea, Peadar's hand freezes as he hears a faint scratching at the door.

Eyes blinking rapidly to clear them of any moisture, Peadar smooths his tunic with shaky hands before opening the cabin door.

Naked and as beautiful as ever, she stands there gazing up at him for several seconds before closing the short distance between them and hugging Peadar fiercely. Hesitantly, Peadar wraps his arms around Shadow and leads her inside.

Hours later, with the full moon high in the sky and the dying embers in the fireplace casting a faint glow within the cabin, the intertwined bodies separate as Peadar rises and pads over to the fire and stirs the embers. His back to the bed, he speaks.

"What's so wrong with me wanting to spend time with you? There are so many experiences we could be sharing together, not just these three days a month stuck in here."

When no answer is immediate, Peadar looks back to see if Shadow had heard and sees her eyes staring back at him, bright and shining in the firelight. Finally she speaks. "Don't I make you happy? You enjoy our games, right? What more could you want?"

"Shadow, there is a whole world out there I would like to see with you, I've read of places in my books that I can barely believe, and I'm sure there are wonders out in the wilderness you could show me. Our lives could be so much more than this."

"Squiggles on a page, they mean nothing. The world is what you can hunt, kill, and eat, and we have all that here; why would I want to go anywhere else? My Pack is here, this is where I belong."

"Well then, can't I be part of the Pack?" Peadar asks, a hint of pleading in his tone.

"They would never accept you; there is too much bad blood between man and wolf."

"But what if you spoke on my behalf? You know that I can be trusted, that I love nature as much as you do, I help keep the area safe." Silence answers him. "But you won't do that will you?" Peadar says softly to himself, feeling a part of his soul wither and die.

Arms outreached and sly smile on her face, Shadow purrs, "Come here and let me make you feel better, my strong warrior."

A few short days later, the nightly ritual begins again. The she-wolf Shadow, black as midnight emerges from the forest and tops the rise above the tiny cabin. About to howl out her nightly greeting to her playmate, the she-wolf senses something wrong down at the tiny clearing and goes to investigate.

Padding across the clearing towards the cabin, Shadow finds it dark and hollow; the spark of life that made it the den of the man is gone, only the husk remains. The door stands open but no light spills out and the scent of the man is old. Slipping through the open doorway, the she-wolf sees the empty shelves where beloved books once lived, all other meagre possessions gone as well; the only item left is the remains of a burned bearskin in the fireplace.

Racing outside, Shadow lifts her head to the night's sky and lets of a howl of rage that echoes through the night.

Stacey Oakley

Stacey Oakley is an avid reader and writer, especially of fantasy. She has a Bachelor of Arts in Art History & Visual Studies with a minor in Social Justice Studies from the University of Victoria and is currently in the process of completing a post-grad diploma in Cultural Resource management by distance, also from the University of Victoria. While originally from Moncton, New Brunswick she's lived on both sides of the country, having spent a number of years in British Columbia and only recently moved to Newfoundland.

The following piece of flash fiction, "The Sorrows of War," appears here in print for the first time.

The Sorrows of War

Lightning crashed over the battlefield as the opponents stared each other down atop the cliff, separate from the chaos of the battle below. They didn't want any interruptions for this fight. Both wore heavy armour with the insignia of commander. Neither flinched as rain began to pour in heavy sheets, quickly soaking through everything, mixing with the red earth below to create macabre rivers that ran through trenches and craters, giving bodies movement mimicking life. Red eyes glowed viciously while green eyes shimmered like malevolent emeralds in the flashes of sudden light, vibrant against the darkness of the tempest. The only real light was from the lightning, the explosions, and the glow of magic from the chaos around them. They were both prepared to die this day for their causes, if not for their kings. No words were spoken, for they were long past the time for speaking, for negotiations, for reconciliation. Now was the time to choose the victor.

They leapt forward at the same moment, swords clashing, and sparks flying through the air as they danced the bloody dance of war. The song of ringing steel added to the clamour around them. Spells were cast and thrown. It was beautiful, in a terrifying way. Blood soon mixed with the rainwater on the stone as steel and spell found their marks; neither combatant halted to stop the flow, for they knew that to pause for even the barest moment would make it their last. One raised his hand in the air, and lightning crashed to where the other had been a mere breath before, glowing eyes determined. Then he leapt forward, lunging for the kill when his opponent twisted and struck for his side, the blade in his hands glowing with green fire as it came close to striking heavy armour. He dodged, just barely, rolling and coming back to his feet.

Both tried to push the other towards the edge of the cliff, to make them stumble and fall to their deaths amidst the rocks below. This had been going on too long, and both wanted it to end. Now. Not just the battle, but their entire conflict. They paid no mind to the thunder roaring its fury around them, or to the lightning striking to kill just as intently and eagerly as they were. Not even the fierce and howling winds, drawing at their hair and cloaks and trying to drive them both over the cliff gave them pause. Their enmity had reached the point of no return; neither could reconcile with the other and all that was left was death.

For a single moment, several meters apart, they both paused, and looked at one another. They had been great friends once, not so long ago. But now that was ended. Both searched their hearts to see if they truly had it in them to kill the other. For a moment, even the thunder waited, even the wind stilled, and even the battle seemed to be silenced. Everything seemed to wait for what would happen.

The moment ended as they reached the same conclusion and their gazes hardened, their swords lifted, and they both charged. The battle had drawn on too long; they were both tired and wounded. This would be the last strike. In a moment, only the winner would be left standing, and they both knew it. The wind returned more vicious than before, blowing debris all around, as if it were trying to shield the eyes of anyone who might be nearby, as if to protect them from the tragedy about to occur. No one was meant to see something like this, no one was meant to do something like this. The rain fell even harder with strange mercy, as if to drown the sorrows of this place of war and woe. At once, lightning struck the cliff, a magnificent flash, just as the two met in the centre. Thunder exploded outwards, so that, for a moment, everyone was blind and deaf, no matter who they fought for. In the light, there were two fighters standing, so close they could have embraced one another, and it was impossible to tell who was who. The light faded, and the wind carried the thunder away.

One fighter stood, breathing heavily while the other lay at his feet, impaled by a sword and breathless forevermore. The victor went down on one knee, and reached out to the other, and gently closed the green eyes.

"I'm sorry, brother, but it had to end this way," he murmured, then stood, and walked away without looking back, leaving his sword where it was. He didn't want to use it anymore, not after it had the blood of his brother staining its blade. As it was, he would be paying for this for all eternity.

Matthew Daniels

Matthew Daniels was hatched in St. John's, and spent many years stretching his wings between there and Labrador. Once old enough to hunt on his own, he ventured into the realm of the nerd, where he encountered such delights as Sci-Fi on the Rock, *Magic: The Gathering*, and cake pops shaped like piranha plants set in cupcakes coloured like warp pipes. Though he cannot yet breathe fire, he did join the illustrious non-profit organization Sandbox Gaming, helping to raise money for charities across Newfoundland and Labrador. The following story, "Healers' Hoards", is only one of many he has to tell.

Healers' Hoards

He arrived at the village.

He rode on the back of a hay cart. It had been a few hours since the rain, so the sky was a cautious grey. The air, however, was fresh and excited. Tavern keepers might have said that it "woke up the grass."

It would feel good on his feet.

They were bare, and they hung from the rear edge of the cart. They were so caked with dirt that it was hard to tell the hair on them from the cracks in dried mud. Rolled up trousers announced his knees, but the rest of him was hard to see. He wore a large, thin blanket, wrapped around him with great care. Either someone who loved him took pains for his comfort, or he was paranoid of everything outside his skin.

His back was bent. Age? Long labour? A birth gone wrong? With the blanket woven about him with many artful folds, there were too many bumps to tell clothes from bones. His face was so hidden within the cave of his shroud that only the build of his legs and the heaviness of his breathing gave him up as a man.

It was a dirt road. Puddles stabbed sharply at its earthy

tones with the colours of the sky, steel grey and white, here and there some blue. Shrubbery and bushes made up the greenery in the distance. Much of the land on either side of the road was a herd of stones, like lumbering sea creatures swimming in the earth and frozen as their great backs broke the surface. The rest of the ground lusted to be touched. The wooden fences and lines of tilled earth in the distance showed that there were men eager to please.

All of this unfolded behind the cart and in front of the man. He could hear behind him the swaying of wooden signs on small chains, the running feet of children enjoying the mud, men and women talking about the whole world and nothing at all and the milk this year, the clucking of a lone chicken.

"This is my stop," the man called out over his shoulder, reaching a hand from the depths of his coverings to hold to the side of the cart as he turned. His index finger was missing.

The cart stopped, and he jumped down with more control than his bent back would suggest. Sliding down with him was his sword. Less effectively hidden by the blanket than the rest of him, he'd kept it hidden between his body and the side of the cart; it was easy to steal a sword from a sitting man. "Many thanks," he called to the driver as he walked forward at an angle from the cart and the nearest building. His voice was odd, with each syllable stopping as it came out as though he were biting his own words.

The driver said nothing.

There was no need to keep his sword out, so a fold of cloth, which could be easily swept aside if his safety should change, sheltered it. Other than the stares of people unused to strangers, he was assaulted by nothing but the smell of livestock riding a northeasterly wind.

His steps were sturdy and direct, and never once suffered the indignity of a slip in the mud. His back remained bent, but there was the unmistakable weight of power behind his movements. Not age, then. A back wilted by labour would not carry without a cane or walking stick. A hunchback, then. That was what the wives would say to each other later, folding clothes as a reason to take a break from the men.

None of this earned the attention of the man, and yet he was aware of all of it. His attention came to rest upon a rickety thing across the way. It was barely a shack, but it had a door. The only part of it built with intent was the boarding across the windows - boarded from the inside - which was as even and artless as arithmetic; easily witnessed but put to a purpose. In this case, the purpose was to prevent witnessing of anything that went on beyond.

"Ser!" A woman shouted from across the village square, "That 'un's empty, it is!"

He walked right in. No answer for the woman, and no knock. A flick of his ring finger was enough to send the door to behind him.

The light in the room was strange. He noticed this the same moment he became aware of tension in the air and the positions of three men and a woman in the one-room shack. The four people were clearly shocked, but not yet alarmed.

As he spoke, he realized that the strangeness of the light was not that there was a lantern in every corner – it was that there was no outside light. They were certainly thorough. "You are the Healers Four, one for every corner of death." He held up both hands now, palms facing the others in a gesture of peace. Both hands lacked index fingers. "You are long in the finding, and my sword is not meant for you."

"It is not your sword we fear." This was the woman. She sat on a rocking chair, wearing a simple brown dress and a beige shawl. She could have been anyone in the village. Were it not for her presence here, he would not have known her for one of the Four. But then, the men were equally careful not to have particularly distinguishing features. No obvious tattoos, for instance.

"I do not bring fear with me," the intruder answered. He lowered his hands and clasped them in front of him.

"Everyone brings fear with them," answered one of the men. His hair was short and thin: once strong black, but now mostly silvery grey. His eyes were grey as well, and so sharp it was easy to overlook the softness in his voice.

Another of the Four, standing tall with arms as thick as a bear's legs, smiled through his shaggy mass of light brown hair. "You're wondering why we aren't better armed."

"If you know so much of the ways of fear," the intruder confirmed.

The last of the four to speak was crouched by a bag of supplies he had been managing. At first the intruder thought him small, but then the man stood to approach. He was neither tall nor short, but thin as lines and colourful in his style of motion. He put on a show of the small and mouse-like, one it takes a sharp eye to recognize. He was bald, but by design, not age. His nose had a way of twitching that also was not unlike a mouse. "To find us is no easy task. Why all of this trouble, merely to replace lost fingers?"

There was a short chuckle from within the darkness of the cloth folded about the intruder's head. It was blunt and humourless. "Those wounds were by design."

"A warrior," the woman said. "But your skin does not match the yellow of the east. How is it then that you bear their mark, the sacrifice for a stronger grip?"

"I am not here to share my decisions."

"Ah, but you are. That is what the people come to us for. To take the risk that led to harm was a choice. To acknowledge it as harm is a choice. To seek healing is a choice. If you have come to us at all, it is to share your decisions." This came from the thin man.

"Let us begin by the sharing of names," interjected the silver-haired one.

"We are each of us named for the corner of death we explored, the one we specialize in undoing and denying," explained the man like a bear.

"I am Violence," said the woman.

"She is the greatest fighter among us," said the large man, whose arms looked built to bend iron.

"Neglect," the silver-haired man admonished, "Pride leaves a trail."

"Apologies."

Sharp, grey eyes turned to the intruder. "I am Folly, and I am learned in deaths of the mind. I hope you will forgive us if we do not explain Neglect. Some things, when exposed, become all the more hidden."

"If I could rival the wisdom of a healer in his own craft, I would not have sought you out," answered the intruder. He then turned to the thin man. "And you are?"

"Malady."

"These are not names," the intruder pointed out, "but they will do. You may call me Close."

Folly got to the question: "What do you seek from us, Close?" Not one of them asked him about his name, though they explained their own choices. Curious.

Now no longer an intruder, Close set about unraveling himself from the blanket. It was no mere piling-on, but a technique. A cultural sleight of hand, and not learned from his own people; his white skin meant northern climes with mountains. Lands where thick furs and hardy belts built a person up against the cold, and often withstood the rigours of travel better than the person wearing them. Not a place for cloth wraps, no matter how thick, layered, or thorough.

His audience gasped. Standing before them was a man in little more than rags, trousers still folded to the knees and feet filthy. His jaw was chiseled to cut glass, his hair ragged and blond. Brown eyes held a cold fire. But all of these sights were lost to other features.

"To know my need," he said to them, "you must know my tale. I will have your vow not to interrupt me until I have finished the telling."

"An oath from every corner of death is not easily given."

"Nor broken," was his response. He could tell that they were very eager to know this story. Almost desperately so. They swore it, each in turn, and in full; an oath was done properly or not at all. Then he began.

"My story started at a tavern. The Dancing Snake. Its keeper, a man so tall and thin his father must have been a rail, told us all about why he called it that. His mother-in-law loved the idea of something without legs dancing. That's the short answer, at any rate. Took him fifteen minutes to tell us about his wife's shoe collection first. He wasn't quick to the point, that one, and he mixed up the orders more often than not. Still, he'd give you his skin if you had more need of it. You know the sort.

"Now, this barkeep, being that type, made some arrangements. The town was next to a mountain range, and this was normally a good thing. Spring water there was in plenty, and there were some tourist attractions I didn't care about. The Dragon was not a good thing, though. Hard on tourism, and people fear the fires they don't make themselves, if you take my meaning. That's how my story started: I was seated in the tavern with some men who were not gentle, and these men represented...well, they went on about that. Each of them had their own corners, so to speak. They were all there, in a nutshell, to help the barkeep find someone like me.

"They had some money. I wanted money. They needed something dead. I was known as a hero of the war, and not because of my cooking. Business, you understand.

"I told them the truth: mountains are never as close as they seem. It might be some time before I returned. None of these men were spring chickens, so they raised no objections. There was no guarantee I would ever be seen again, of course – no one needed to be told that. So I accepted the arrangement of half up-front and half when I came back with a Dragon's hide in addition to my own. Most of my first half was used to secure resources and make preparations. A large part of that was making arrangements with the inn keeper to have a week's worth of room and board ready for me if I should return for more supplies, recuperation, or the second half of my pay. Everyone was grateful for my help, of course. I did not blame them; even in good times, few people can part with quality gear without compensation and not feel the loss.

"These were not good times.

"Since no one was thrilled to go with me, I was only able to secure enough for one man to carry. This was just as well, because travelling light was the wisdom of my task. To make up for the lack of space available to me, I needed more expensive materials, especially foodstuffs. These mountains would not keep a hungry man going for long. Most importantly, of course, I needed more oil and a better whetstone for my sword, as well as implements for carrying, covering, and cleaning it. All of the utmost quality, naturally. I wouldn't be spreading butter with it.

"You're probably wondering why I wasn't bothering with distance weapons. Very simple: I am a warrior. My sword's importance is a given. But distance weapons are cumbersome, and would have to be custom-designed for a feat like Dragon-slaying. What's more, I knew as much about Dragons as most people do: they kill people. I was a person – more or less – and the role of people is supposed to be turning backs toward Dragons and eagerly exercising leg muscles.

"I would have to study my prey. Watch it from afar, learn when it sleeps – if it sleeps – and be as prepared as possible. I questioned everyone for some distance in and around the town before setting out, so I could learn as much as I could. Apparently, there was a Festival of Learning that happened at a town on the other side of the mountains three times a year. Those festivals always lasted exactly four weeks – twenty-eight days – and not with the months. The timing had nothing to do with the moon or the calendar or any folktales anyone in the region knew about. But when those festivals went on, there was never a thing to be heard about the Dragon.

"After the festivals was another matter. The people also spoke of a library somewhere in the mountains, but no one who had had any connection to it had been heard from once the Dragon started showing up. It was a monastery from 'way back when,' or so some of them thought. Others thought it was a front for a brothel. Who travels treacherous, foodless mountain wastes to pay for primal treatments from people who could be carrying Hell's weight in disease? I hear men will go to great lengths for such things. When I was younger, I lived more for wine and war, myself.

"I still love wine. The red, if you have any. Dry as a bone, that's how I like it.

"Most would have made every effort to get a horse to get them so far. Go for the library, that was the natural plan. I needed to learn more one way or another, so I'd have the books if the place wasn't burnt to the ground. Assuming they'd have pictures I could follow, and be in a language someone in town could read. And that there wouldn't be a Dragon waiting for me with seasonings at the ready. But it was just as likely I'd have to go off the beaten path, where no horse could follow.

"And I did. For shelter, if nothing else. My second day into the mountains lasted about thirty-six hours but sleeping alone under the stars in rock country is an excellent one-way ticket to the afterlife. Dragon or no.

"Once I found a fairly high crag that offered a good view, I discovered the library easily enough. This was the fifth day of travelling the rock country, and the library was built into the mountainside some ways ahead. It looked to be half a day's journey, but I have spoken before about the closeness of mountains.

"Earlier that day I met a man who was not afraid in a small wooded glade in a dip near a sheer cliff. He was friendly enough, and shared a stew that had surprising body and flavour. He ate of it first, so I thought it was trustworthy enough. I caught him in lies half a dozen times, though. I did not tarry. He called himself a merchant, so I took him to be a thief – this was no road for trade. It was also no place for lawmen, being so far from the town and so near the Dragon. He could take nothing from me, but I spent the rest of my travels to the library watching for signs of being followed. I found none.

"The library had large double doors. Like the mountain in which it was set, it was mostly stone grey and sharp-edged. Yet it made excellent use of archways, buttresses, and sloped roofs. A landslide didn't seem likely, but they were prepared for it. I know little of building, for warriors are practiced in unmaking, but age and intention are other matters. This was a place that was made to last, and it was made with the kind of love that keeps a sword simple, strong, and sharp.

"Be they man or woman, few could have opened those doors without help. Once inside, there were small rooms built with holes whose purposes I could not divine. There were many gates and strange turns before I could come to any room with meaning. This building was not conceived as a library. It smelled of fresh meat and fire, but not of cooking. I thought this strange.

"Then I found a vast chamber. There were desks in rows that spanned the extent of my vision – which was not great. The only lit torch was my own. Why keep books in so much darkness? The walls were lined with shelves. Both desks and shelves had their books chained to them. This was no surprise; books are not easily crafted, and to those who possess the skill to make use of them, their value is great. So great that there is money to be had. Books I do not understand, but money is another matter.

"A woman was in that room. Her first words to me were, 'Good evening, and morning, and everything between.' As she came closer, she asked fearlessly, 'What good were you hoping to do with a sword, in a place like this?'

"In return for her hospitality, I pointed out that a desk had a lonely chain on it. There was sadness in her as she acknowledged this, and stepped into the light of my torch. The sadness was not her tone, nor her expression. She wore it like clothes, heavier than the off-white robe. She was ill, or perhaps tired.

"She called herself Opus, but this was not her name. She had a little more weight than she needed to give her curves, with straight blond hair and brown eyes. To measure her by sizes and lines, textures and lengths, many might think her plain. A man who takes such measures would never have seen how beautiful she was. Poets and bards spend their entire lives, sometimes, trying to describe the beauty of someone they love. Our story is not yours to know, and it did not happen at first sight, but this much is important: you know you love someone when you can discover them all over again. I have found nothing, nowhere, and no one else that can be so re-discovered.

"I stayed with her, and soon lost all track of time. Days are meaningless when every moment is new. She often spoke of secrets, and kept many. I ate from a small garden in an enclosure on the east side of the building. I hadn't seen it from the side that I had approached, but I probably wouldn't have anyway – it was higher up into the mountainside than the double-doored entrance. This garden was not well kept, and I am no gardener. I would go out to hunt sometimes. Perhaps Opus did not like that I was out, perhaps it was the hunting. Hunting in the mountains means treacherous footfalls, the surprise discovery that your prey is not alone, and inviting other predators with the smells of blood and meat. But I am well travelled, and this was not the first time I spent many days away from inns or cooks.

"She would eat from the fruits of my labours, but always I sensed she did so to appease me. Her condition did not worsen, did not improve. We often found that silence was as meaningful as speech, and a lack of words between us did not change our comfort and simple delights. I made dolls for her, a skill I learned while working as a mercenary in a land of farms and tall grasses. Learn to love children and people are more free with their money, their food, their roofs.

"Their beds.

"I am a quick study, it seems. That woman loved to teach, to share. She was not the sort to judge someone as unknowing, or to attack with facts. She just liked to talk about things that are new – if not to herself, then to her audience. Stories were a passion for her, as much as secrets.

"We shared many. Stories, that is. She had a fondness for tea. That part of the garden she cared deeply for. I learned to work with the fruits and vegetables based on what she taught me of the tealeaves.

"But it weighed upon me that she remained unwell, and so very troubled about that missing book. I brought it up often, and when we argued, that was the subject. During those times I could go outside, roam, train. I found signs of the Dragon. Old scales, mostly. Occasional marks in stones from talons. A stretch of stone that had been melted into a pool. Only Dragon fire, so far as I know, can do such things. Naturally, I asked her about it. Or to teach me anything that might be in the books. She said none of them were about Dragons.

"'But I've seen pictures of them. Here, like this one,' I told her once, showing her a book I'd noticed.

"'Oh, that's a book of poetry. About beasts.'

"'Dragons are not beasts.' It took me a long time to understand her smile about that.

"She never did give me a straight answer about the Dragon. It was clear that it had been nearby. One time, I decided I'd get one. An answer. I didn't, but I pushed until she finally stood and said, 'Come with me.'

"She led me far down into basement levels, where I

would not have guessed a building could go. I suspect you four would have liked this library, so deep and dark and full of things unknown. If you can heal me, I will tell you how to get there. Anyway, the air was thicker so far underground, like it was becoming the soil that surrounded it. There was more moisture than I would have expected. I have rarely had cause to be so far beneath the surface of the earth.

"I was soon lost, and glad of her guidance. She was quiet for most of the walk, so the heavy smell of dark places held us and pulled us, much like the weight of our breathing. 'In secrets there is great power,' she said suddenly, as we neared the end of a spiraling staircase.

"I said nothing. This was a lesson, it seemed.

"Sure enough: 'A secret can open doorways otherwise closed to us. It can be a frightful weapon. Oft, it is the arrow that finds meat for a man's family. But a weapon, nonetheless.'

"'Is that why you share so few secrets with me?'

"'Are you asking about the doorways or the weapons?' She didn't bother looking at me as she spoke.

"'Both.'

"Again, her smile. It was different from the smile she shared during... secret moments. I am still uncertain if it was a doorway or a weapon.

"We came upon a wall at the end of a corridor. At the time I wondered, Who goes to the trouble of building a deep underground hall with no purpose at its end?

"She said, 'I will share with you the secret of the Healers Four.' And she did.

"Now, there are feats that seem like magic. These are

achieved with distraction, with tricks of the light, or with skillful hands. Until I saw that door open at the end of that corridor, I did not believe in magic. I lack the knowledge to tell you why, but I knew that no mechanism of wood, metal, or stone could have moved that doorway.

"'How can you know such things? The Healers Four, and...' I pointed at the door with the three fingers of one hand. Sign language can be surprisingly challenging without the pointing fingers, but she took my meaning easily enough.

"'It's a secret,' she said with a grin. Her voice resonating in that deep place added to her body. Music and flesh. We had another secret moment then, amid the moist stones and darkness. I could feel a power at work that I did not understand, and there were corners in me that knew fear.

"Beyond the Secret Door there was a vault. Stone tablets were kept there. The moist atmosphere would not have been good for books, even I could see that. She showed me markings on these tablets, and gave me a long lesson that I found hard to follow. I came to understand that the missing volume I'd noticed in the room of desks was important for using these tablets. It was of great importance to her, that book. Just what the tablets were for wasn't clear to me, but I understood that there was power in them. They were tied to the doorway we'd come through in some way that could not be seen.

"'These tablets can reveal secret powers to me, then,' I said.

"'To us,' Opus corrected.

"'Then I shall find the volume.'

"I was surprised by the despair in her eyes. 'You would know the Dragon, still?'

"'I am a man of my word, secrets or no,' I answered. I did not ask why she would talk about knowing and not killing.

"She did not stop me from leaving, but I could tell a great weight was upon her. She needed that book with something more than homesickness and less than hunger. But she did not want me to pursue it.

"I went in search of the man who was not afraid. I had no trouble finding him; a man who does not live in fear does not hide his tracks.

"After I explained myself, he said, 'For three payments, I will take you to where you need to go.'

"'It is not a place that I seek,' I said.

"He laughed. 'Every seeker is looking for a place. It may not be a place you can touch, that you can taste, smell, see, or hear. But it is a place.'

"Not a thief, then. Thieves are masters of fear, always navigating the risk of getting caught and the chance that what had value one moment will not the next. To master fear, one must live in it. Always.

"(I remind you of your oaths.)

"He brought me to a place of ruined stone pillars, about a day's march from the library. 'The first price is copper,' he said when we arrived.

"Fair enough. I paid him in money. That's a price I understand.

"In the ruins there was a stone well. There were some frogs. 'Do not harm them,' the man who was not a merchant said to me.

"'I had no intent-'

"'You do not understand,' and he stopped fast to level his gaze upon me. 'Be vigilant. Take care not to step on them. Be mindful of your sword. If you throw a stone, aim it far from them.'

"I thought this very odd, but I nodded agreement to his terms. Why, I still do not understand, but there is more to living – and surviving – than understanding.

"We came to the well. I rested my hands upon it. Cautiously, with eyes and ears on the alert for any sudden movements of the frogs, I looked into the water. I saw water.

"'Things may be hidden in water,' he said to me.

"'Things may be hidden anywhere,' I answered.

"'Very true!' he said with a laugh. 'But there is a secret to hiding in water.' He looked me over then, and there was something in his eyes that I did not trust. 'And I see that you are not unfamiliar with secrets.'

"I narrowed my eyes. 'What is the price?'

"'Air. To hide in water, one must pay the price of wind.'

"'Breathing is important to me,' I objected.

"He only grinned. 'Naturally. I wouldn't have it any other way. But death is never payment. No, to pay this price, you must share a story with me.'

"'A story?' And then I stepped back. 'I see. You are a madman. I am wasting my time.'

"He closed his eyes. Still closed, he spoke. 'Are you so sure?' He unleashed his gaze once more, and held me with it. 'Look at the well again.'

"I did. The book was there, floating just under the

surface. I was horrified. 'I thought you were speaking in riddles! The book is ruined!'

"'No.'

"Frustrated, I moved to take it from the water. The image rippled as my hand closed over water, and nothing more. But to look at the book, it was clearly there. A hand span from the surface.

"'There are secrets in stories, traveller.'

"'There are secrets in everything,' I said, exasperated.

"He truly looked surprised. 'Too true. You are wiser than your sword suggests.'

"'It is unwise to mock a man with a weapon.'

"'Do you truly know so little of swords that you would try to cut mockery with one?'

"When he said that, I became a little afraid, I must confess. I felt like he could see into places in me where he had no business looking. Merchants can have an incredible understanding of the shallow places in a person, but rarely do they see deeper. This man was no merchant.

"'Does my choice of story matter?' I did not look away from the book that was and was not in the water of the well. There was a croak next to my sword hand, still resting on the stone edge. I ignored it.

"'The one you have chosen does not. But that it is one you chose? Absolutely. Yes.' No, then.

"I assumed that the story would have more power if it were more than just a passing thing. More than a tavern joke or a roadside yarn. So I told the story of when I first learned to make dolls. You don't need to know that story.

"When I finished, the book rose out of the water, floating on the surface. I picked it up. It was heavy, undamaged, dry. I looked at the man who had no fear.

"'I claimed that book when I took it from the library,' the man said.

"'You have no claim to a stolen thing. That is what stealing means.'

"'There is much that you do not know, wise swords-man who is not of the east.'

"'I am no longer interested in your riddles. I got what I came for.' I turned to go.

"'There was a reason I named three prices,' he said. He was in no rush. I was so surprised by the ease of his tone that I turned around.

"'For you to keep what you have found after I have laid claim to it, I must pay the price of dust.' He waited while I stared him down. I have met few who could stand up to the full force of my glare. Not because I am boastful, but because of the things I have kept in my eyes.

"'...and what is the price of dust?' I asked once it was clear I could not overpower him.

"'I love the roads, traveller. That is why I live on them. That is why you found me in a place that was no one's home. I do not claim home. I wander. But I need your help to pay the price of dust, to give up the roads.'

"I stared at him. 'That is why you took the tome. You've been waiting for someone to come claim it.'

"'There is power in it, yes.' That was all that he would say.

"'I cannot read,' I admitted. Without shame.

"'I can teach you the passages you will need. Simply reading out the words, after all, will have no effect. You must understand their full meaning, and your own intent.'

"'Few know the full meaning of their own intentions. I have travelled enough to know this,' I replied.

"He laughed again. I was learning to dislike that laugh. I am, after all, a quick study. 'You need only know the full meaning of the words. I do not expect you to understand the full meaning of your intention in reading them.'

"'I do not trust you,' I said to this.

"'No one does,' he answered. Despair lined his lips like a forbidden drink. But not, I think now, because of absent trust.

"He taught me the passage. It took until nightfall. I was required to go away from him to read it. Why, I did not know. No frogs were harmed, for what that's worth.

"Once I had left the perimeter of the ruins, well out of sight of him, I opened the book and read it aloud by moonlight. By the time I finished, I could taste road dust in my mouth. I felt as though I had travelled by moonlight. This was a thing I did not understand.

"But the words I understood. I had read a curse. To keep the book, I had to place a curse upon him, that he may never travel again. Any attempt to leave the perimeter – outlined by the ruins – would be met with dust before being restored to his point of origin.

"Then the night screamed.

"Caught off guard, horrified by what I might have done, I dropped the book and ran back to the ruins.

"There was a dragon. Its scales gleamed in the moonlight. Brown, I thought. Or maybe the greys, blacks, silvers, reds, and browns of gravel roads. Perhaps the light green of a path in the woods. Colour is a secret of light, and moonlight is a tricky thing. The scales surprised me the most, because they weren't lined up like people in an army formation. They were like pebbles: all of a different size and shape, but none overwhelming to its neighbours. Like a walkway constructed with ordered intent to resemble chaos.

"I could not see its eyes from where I was standing. I did not know a neck could twist and bend and wrap about the air in such a way and not cause harm to the head it bears. Rounded bumps of bone adorned its skull in an oval shape, with a larger bump in the middle. There were similar bone patterns at the elbows and knees. Its claws were like a bear's. There were three tails, long and thin and tipped with a spade shape. There were three tongues and many teeth in its mouth.

"I have seen elephants in my travels back from the east. This creature could have wrestled an elephant and won.

"At least, if it were healthy.

"It made dashes for the perimeter of the ruins. Twice it flew over my head. Always it was brought back to where the man had been standing, by the well. It was in great pain, yet it took care not to step on the frogs or sweep them away with its wings or tails. With every attempt at travel that it took, it returned with greater wounds.

"It lay there on the ground before me when it was spent. There was sharpness in its gaze that I recognized. Its eyes were not slits, but had yellow circles in them like the bone bumps; smaller circles in an oval with a larger yellow one in the middle. Its breath was ragged. Blood flowed along the contours of its body like streams on the bodies of mountains. It spoke:

"'I love the roads. But death is never payment.'

"'Are you...' I said as I approached, '...the man without fear?'

"It coughed blood as he laughed. Yes, I definitely disliked that laugh. 'Without fear. I thought you were wise?'

"'I never made that claim.'

"'Wise.'

"'Why did you plague the mountains and people?' I asked. I knew it was a childish question. Like asking a wolf why it has fangs.

"I did not understand at the time what the look in his eyes meant. I know now. He didn't understand my question. He didn't know what I was asking, or what I was talking about.

"After a pause, and as his eyes were drooping with his last breaths, I looked around. I regretted leaving Opus' prized book on the ground, though why that came to mind just then, I didn't know. Still, I looked around. I frowned. 'Don't Dragons have hoards?'

"That blasted laugh. 'You...expect...gold?' He wheezed at the end of that.

"'There are other hoards?'

"I was surprised by the road dust that covered him, now that I was so close. And looking. I'd have thought all that flying would have dusted him off. Unless it was the dust from the curse? But why wasn't there any on the well, or on the frogs?

"Come to think of it, where were the frogs?

"What was a Dragon fell apart before me, into dust and the splintered wood of road signs, spines falling off and becoming bootstraps, twigs, simple utensils, and other things a person might bring on the road. His wings became a tattered travelling cloak. Now he truly was the ruined body of the man without fear.

"I didn't think he answered my question when he said: 'A Dragon's weakness is its heart.'

"He never laughed again.

"I returned to Opus with the volume. She never told me what she did with it, but I never saw it again. We went on to be happy together. I knew I could return to town now for payment, but I was in no rush. I have no idea how long we stayed like that. There was more than one language in the texts to be found in that library, so she picked one – the one I speak – to teach me the reading of it.

"I never enjoyed reading. I did it for her. It seemed to matter to her. At the time, I couldn't guess why. I stopped telling her that my hands were for swords, not the turning of pages, because it would put sadness in her eyes. I could lose myself in those eyes, so I did not want to see sadness there. It is like getting lost in a place you've known your entire life because you have never seen it in darkness, and so the turns and walls have changed shape before you.

"So I would only pick up a tome once every few days, and read a few pages until I felt sure I had read enough to satisfy her – even if she was not there to see it, and never checked to see how much I'd covered. In all, I read twelve books. There were times when she said she had to go to a task, and asked me not to emerge from deep within the library until she returned to me. I did not understand this:

"'You will be unguarded,' I said to her.

"'I have lived here for years, my close one, and long

before the rumours of the Dragon came about.' This she said with a curled smile, like a kitten playing with yarn.

"'They were not rumours!' And she knew the meaning of this, that I would be paid for the task.

"'Ah, but they were rumours,' she answered. 'That they were true does not change their nature.'

"And that was how it was. She never accepted my offers to teach her in the arts of combat. Do not look at me so; combat can be more an art than healing, as it leaves many kinds of marks that cannot be undone.

"Always she would say, 'Happy I am to learn many things. But this is not a thing for me.'

"Always when she returned, she would smell of meat and fire – but not cooked meat. There was an energy about her that allowed for no questions, and only once did I go against this. I never got the answers I sought.

"After a while, she started moving some wheelbarrows into the large room with the desks. There were odd places for some of these where she needed my help. The places were convenient for getting the size of the wheelbarrows out of the way, but how did one of them get up three indentations in the stone walls, which were used in most other places for books or small tools? I saw no pulleys or special ladders.

"Perhaps, when it was a monastery, strong monks might have gotten up on ladders and shared the burden, lifting it by either end with one hand while the other stayed upon the ladder. But again, it was odd – and a remarkable feat of strength.

"Anyway, I helped her put many of the books into these wheelbarrows. She said that the thieves of the last time (I never told her exactly how I got the tome back) had been weighing upon her mind. She wanted the books moved to a safer place. So we gathered them all near the front gate, in five large wheelbarrows. I wasn't sure what her plan was. We could not move them down the stairs in wheelbarrows, so we could not go into the depths below. Which was just as well, since the books wouldn't last long in the moisture.

"The book she used to teach me to read was about swordsmanship, to keep my interest. The first book she had me read on my own was about book maintenance. We had an argument because of that. I felt she was leading me by the nose, and...

"...nevermind. I should not tarry in this tale. The end will not change merely by lengthening the telling.

"When we had them all arranged, we fully closed the front gates. We set up the crossbeams to fall into place when we closed them, walling out intruders. She said she had a secret way back in, which no one else could violate, and that I would understand in the morning.

"She had another secret to tell me.

"We walked, slowly. Enjoying the evening and each other. We spent that night near a hot spring she showed me. Many were the secret moments we shared that night. She said that this was the place of her birth. I liked it there. It was sheltered. The air was cool and the water was warm. It was a place for poetry and movement, despite its stillness. But no weapon did I bring there.

"I woke the next morning to birdsong and the glow of sunlight at the rocky edges of the cavern of the hot spring. And I knew something was wrong. Opus was nowhere to be seen.

"I made a mad dash for the library, because I could see smoke there once I emerged from the cavern and grabbed my sword. Even going as fast as I could, it took me more than an hour to get there, at a guess. There were bodies. I couldn't identify them because I had neither time nor distance.

"I was coming down from the eastern side of the library's gates, so I did not see until I rounded the incline of the mountain that the gates had been melted into a hardened-liquid hole. The Dragon was well away from me, on the western side of the gates, fighting a group I could not see from there. Not well enough to know them.

"Then a familiar voice among them shouted: 'I told you sending a lone man was madness!' It was the innkeeper. From the town. The rest of them must have been townspeople.

"As I ran past the hole that was the gates, a blaze caught the corner of my eye. Dread filled me as I looked and saw a badly-burned man setting fire to the wheelbarrows of books. 'Light' was all I could hear him saying, over and over, as he crumbled to the floor. He was fumbling with his side, and in his condition, the sunlight beyond the ruined gate must have seemed a journey of many leagues.

"Half the thought of what this would mean to Opus came into my head before the scream of the Dragon drove everything else out. It had turned, ignoring the townspeople, and I stood there. My sword in my hand. Fire bursting forth from the creature that stood before me. But not from its maw.

"Strange writing swirled and etched the edges of the

Dragon. The bones of the wings, the boundaries of its spines. Adorning its head like a crown. Its underbelly and the flesh of its wings were a yellow-white, like the pages of a tome. Its scales were an inky black, and almost shimmered with wetness. Its tail, wrists, ankles, and long neck had a strange metallic mane that looked a lot like the chains on the books in the library.

"Lines of fire emerged from all of these places. Bits of flesh flew away from it not as you would expect, but as ash. As though the Dragon were made of paper or wood. The townspeople stopped attacking as they saw the ashes go up in a cloud.

"I ran forward, into the cloud, and my sword fell to my side. Opus lay in my arms. Her eyes were open, but they were closed to the world. I looked back, then. At the library with the smoke of the burning books sneaking out from near the roof like a guilty child getting out of his room through the window. I remembered the words of the man without fear:

"A Dragon's weakness is its heart."

He arrived at the end of his tale.

He was standing. Just as he was at the beginning of the tale. On a box next to tall, bear-like Neglect is an empty wineskin. It had been full, the wine red, but the Healers Four had obliged Close's request as he spoke. They had also been true to their oaths, and had not interrupted. So he stood before them, in nothing but a pair of old pants rolled up to the knees. He was aware of many things.

"This is not how you started to become a Dragon," Malady said. The flighty, mouse-like man spoke with a high pitch and rubbed his hands in a nervous, rolling way.

Close was aware of the vial the instant it was in Malady's hand; while it was not a blade, there were only so many ways a hand can grasp a weapon.

It was a kind of green, wrought of living things and meant for the killing of things. Like disease.

Close was aware of the shack's door behind him. It opened inward; he would not be able to dash out before the healers could set upon him, especially not bent as he was. That bend came from new bones in his back. The beginnings of wings. These, too, pressed upon his knowing. He was aware of his teeth, all incisors now. The smell of meat and wine on his breath. The shape of his nose, lower now and moving to connect with his mouth with every new dawn.

Even were he to pass the threshold, he would be faced with villagers who, seeing his countenance, would name him Fear. Death. Pain. Darkness. Things that were always too close. And yet, they would close in upon him. Of this, he was aware.

In his mind's eye, Close envisioned himself on his knees at the spring. His sword's tip facing himself. His memory returned to the present. He did not answer the question Malady did not quite ask.

"He cannot tell us what he does not know," Folly said, scolding again. No one in the room doubted that he was speaking to Malady, but he kept his eyes on Close. Folly's blade was a stick of chalk. In the other hand was a slate. Close saw him produce these items, but did not know what use they would have now.

Violence was the only one to brandish a weapon that Close did not see coming. It was on her lap, not even in her hands. A knife made of many things, divided and uncouth. Obsidian, steel, bone, even rock. Tools of violence, unfit for such a union. Yet strangely fitting on the lap of this older woman. Her hands rested on the arms of her chair, but he was no fool; she was not as restful as she looked. She was the obvious choice for attack. He did not intend to choose her first. She spoke:

"You have come to us seeking help. Yet there are many kinds of help. Some of them are dangerous, as you learned at the well with the frogs."

Neglect was the last of the Four to speak: "There must be many secrets in the flesh of a Dragon." His hands were empty, but that emptiness may very well have been his weapon.

In a house of healing, the sliding song of Close's sword rang clean and with a kind of love. "I am not a Dragon yet."

Darren Hann

Darren Hann grew up in the small town of Old Shop, leaving at age eighteen and moved to Mount Pearl, where he has resided since. In 2006, Darren co-founded the Sci-Fi on the Rock convention, bringing a never before seen celebration of science fiction and fantasy to Newfoundland.

His first short story, "The Time Diamond", appeared in the original *Sci-Fi from the Rock*, published in April 2010. The following story, "Holy Troll", is a fan-favourite first published in *Sci-Fi from the Rock Returns*.

Holy Troll

"Master, get up!" said the little man. "The battle is lost. We are doomed. The Romans have defeated our army, and we must run and hide."

"You are a good companion, my little Ryloc," said the battle weary solider, Ja-Ramas.

"Sire, follow me," the little man said as he helped his master to his feet and into a musty hole in the cliff. Too small to call a cave, it would now prove to be a haven, a shelter from the Roman army.

"Here, my Ryloc, we shall stay until the Roman army moves on," groaned Ja-Ramas as he started to tend to the many wounds he received during the last battle.

After seeing to Ja-Ramas' needs, Ryloc looked to his master for guidance. "Master, the night grows cold and I am hungry; shall I go look for food and fire? After all, a good servant's first and only duty is to his master's care, and not his own."

"We will find food in the morning, Ryloc. Tonight, let us take what rest we can."

With that, Ja-Ramas bedded down for the night. The next morning, he rose and paused when he heard a loud but comforting voice, one he had heard many times before.

"Go forth to the City of Nul. There you will find a man named Issical, he will provide you with the weapons you need to carry on the fight for your people."

As the voice faded, Ja-Ramas went in search of his manservant. "Come, Ryloc, it is time to leave this place. It has served its purpose."

"But, master, we still have need of food, and you are still recovering from your wounds."

"That will wait, for now I suddenly feel stronger, as if I have been given a new life by some higher power."

"Yes, master," Ryloc reluctantly agreed. "I am, as always, your servant."

They left the cavern as the dawn approached over the quiet field that just last night was the stage for so much bloodshed. Many bodies from both sides of the battle lay dead, but Ja-Ramas and his servant rode through the carnage oblivious to it all. They crested the top of one hill, then another, and another. Finally with the battlefield many miles behind them, they came upon the City of Nul.

A low, stone building stood to the right of the road. Venturing up to it, they were met at the entrance by a tall man wearing a robe made from the skins of many desert animals. He looked them over.

"I am Issical," he said in a very deep voice. "I have weapons and supplies for you, but you can each only take two items with you, for that is the law."

All his life Ryloc had followed these rules. He supposed his master knew what he was doing, for he always heard the voice of the Holy Power in his head leading him to the next great battle.

"Come, Ryloc, we have to move on," Ja-Ramas said.

"But, master, we need rest," insisted Ryloc.

"You are a very wise man, my servant. We shall pause here for tonight, then resume our travels again in the morning."

Day broke and Ryloc rushed to ready their horses. He knew the trip back to their home would be a long and dangerous one, and as he and his master were the only survivors of the battle, he knew they would be sought after still by their enemies. The Romans had a habit of knowing how many men and how much equipment their enemies always had and whether or not every casualty was accounted for. Scouts would be sent to hunt down any survivors and eliminate them. When a Roman army won a battle, they left no survivors.

In the mid-morning of the second day of their new quest, Ryloc realized how tired the horses were. "Master Ja-Ramas, the horses need rest; may we stop, sir?"

"Is it the horses, Ryloc, or is your bottom weary from the ride?"

"No sir. They are weary, may we stop and rest?"

"So be it."

As Ja-Ramas dismounted his brutish warhorse with its coat as white as snow and Ryloc dismounted his small mottled gray pony, they both heard chains rattling and horse hooves pounding the dry desert soil. Both looked up to the small ridge in front of them.

Ja-Ramas cocked his head to the side and Ryloc looked at him curiously. "What is it, master? Is it the voice in your head again?

"Yes, my friend, my saviour is telling me to look under the rocks on the other side of this ridge to the right. We will find something there to help us."

"Master, this voice you keep hearing, it scares me at times. But I know you have heard it all your life and so if you trust in it then so must I."

Ja-Ramas walked around to the other side of the mound of sand and spotted a rattlesnake.

"What good is a snake in a fight, sire?" asked Ryloc.

"Horses are afraid of snakes, my little friend," said Ja-Ramas as they both realized that the noise of the chain and hooves pounding had stopped. Ja-Ramas looked to his left. He raised his big boot and with a hard but firm kick sent Ryloc flying to land almost ten feet away just before a large length of chain smashed the ground where the little man had been standing.

Ryloc hit the ground hard and rolled; this was not the first time his master has flung him to safety. He turned to see a Roman solider, wearing a suit of chain, raise a sword to strike at his master. "What kind of manservant would I be if my master died while in my charge?" he thought.

Ryloc rummaged frantically through the satchel he wore slung over his shoulder. In it he found one of the two items he was allowed to take from Issical's stores. It was a sling, a simple but effective weapon that a man need not have height or strength to use. He reached down and felt through the sand to find a suitable stone. Placing the stone in the sling, he twirled it around and around over his head, then released one end to let the stone fly.

It flew straight and true, through the air and toward

its target until it hit the hunter in the back. He had aimed for the man's head but hitting his back would still cause a fair amount of pain and distraction. The hunter quickly turned to look his attacker straight in the eyes, but to his surprise looked down to see Ryloc looking back up at him. The hunter, more than twice Ryloc's height smirked at Ryloc in disgust at his physical stature. He then raised his large left arm while making a fist to smash Ryloc into the ground. Ryloc covered his head with his hands and looked to the ground, knowing his end was at hand, when a small, bright red drop of blood fell to the ground from the hunter's mouth. The hunter looked confused at first, then his face contorted in pain as Ja-Ramas' sword exploded from his chest.

Ja-Ramas struggled to pull out the sword he had buried hilt deep through the Roman hunter. "Are you well, Ryloc?" he asked.

"Yes, my master, but we must develop a better signal between us for approaching danger. These kicks are beginning to happen far too often."

A smile crossed Ja-Ramas' face. He paused just before he was about to speak and looked up. "Oh no," Ryloc said to himself. "The Holy voice again."

"Continue on to the city of Gault, Ja-Ramas. There you will find solders to accompany you back to the battle. First though, you must pass three wells. Drink the holy water from each well and it will stop your thirst after you leave the city."

"What now, master, another message?" asked Ryloc.

"Yes and I know now where to find help. Let us proceed at once."

They mounted their horses and started on their way.

After many miles they found the first well and Ja-Ramas drank from it, encouraging Ryloc to do the same. Later they came upon the second well, then the third. At each, they paused to drink. Eventually they came to the gates of the city where Ja-Ramas knocked on the giant wooden doors. A lone old man walked out of a small section of one of the doors to greet them.

"We seek passage, elder," Ja-Ramas said.

"Have you completed your holy quests?" the elder asked.

"What do you know of our quests, old man?" asked Ja-Ramas.

"I know you had to fight in the war, you had to pick only two holy weapons to protect you on your journey. I know of the wells you had to drink from..."

Before the old man could continue, a spear flew over Ryloc's head just missing him but striking its target. Another Roman hunter had followed them to Gault and his spear now pierced Ja-Ramas' torso, its bloodied tip pinning him to one of the large wooden doors that protected the city.

Ryloc was looking up at his master's face when he noticed a face looking down from the sky. This then must be where the holy messages always came from that his master heard. He also noticed something written in the clouds beneath the face.

PLAYER ONE IS DEAD.

GAME OVER.

Larry Gent

A Perth, Ontario native, Larry Gent currently resides in Halifax with his wife Valerie.

Mirrored Blade
The Hellguard Scrolls

In the night of fate, when hell poured out,
And the forces of evil marched without doubt,
When the heroes of light fought to the last man,
But the forces of good lost their last stand.
When the civilized world burn to the ground
In the flame of that night, evil was crowned.

These chilling words were known across the globe; each terrifying verse was taught to students, each sonnet muttered by minstrels and bards, and each word forlornly sung by mariachis. The war poem, fabricated by the famously illiterate soldier Charrin Toolicar, signified the change the world went through a decade earlier. Venter Zug knew the war poem by heart; it meant more to him than most people. The world changed for everybody on that fateful night, but none more than him and his Hellguard platoon.

Every time he stood before a group of new recruits, he repeated those words: a chilling reminder of what they getting into. For a decade, Venter and the Hellguard had fought tirelessly against the fiendish forces, fighting them back and keeping them locked into Hellhold, but their numbers were dwindling. The Hellguard needed more warriors.

"Ten years ago, the gates of hell opened and legions of demons and devils poured out into our world, into the capital city of Wyrnica." Venter tried to look stoic, wearing his trusted, albeit worn armour, but his old bones felt tired and weary. "Terafanis was the great empire that stood undefeated for a hundred years. It fell to the hellish invasion in a mere ten days."

"Why are you telling us this?" a voice cried out from the recruits. "We all know this. Why repeat it?"

"You all know these facts, everybody does, but you will each learn to live it." The old recruiter eyed his new soldiers, fighters and warriors from all walks of life. He saw a northerner, thieves from the Enclave, barbarians looking for fame, and even one of the Beastmen tribes, a Bearling. Soon, if the living god was willing, this ragtag assemblage of misfits would become brothers and sisters. "When the great empire fell, and dozens of kingdoms became free, nobody had the resources to fight the hellions, nobody save for the Hellguard. The forces of hell have made Wyrnica into Hellhold, their foothold, and we intend to keep them there. The Hellguard patrol the free kingdoms, we hunt the forces of darkness, and we send them back to the hell from which they came. The forces of hell never give up and neither do we."

The last words echoed in the great hall, the stone monument a droplet of history left by the ruins of the *city-that-once-was*. Now this land was Bastion Breath, the home and stronghold of the Hellguard. Stone gryphons, carved high into the stone walls, glared down with watchful eyes and keen ears, as if the avian spirits listened to each word the old battle lord spoke, critiquing him with each stony look.

"Each of you has come here by your own means; each of you has a past, but as of today, none of that matters. Each of you will undergo rigorous training before you even pick up a weapon." Venter eyed his cohorts, each whispering between each other and eagerly waiting the next words. "None of you know how to fight."

Like the red-hot lava erupting from a volcano, rage erupted from the recruits. For the soldiers looking for a home, the knights looking for duty, and the bearling, this declaration was an insult. Each of them were seasoned warriors, their skills honed from countless battles; they were not mere recruits.

"I am Rothgore, Grizzly-Berserker and I am a true warrior!" The Bearling roar was deafening. The Beastmen races were just that, beasts who now shared humanoid traits like intelligence and cunning, yet of the dozens of beast species that emulated the higher forms, none were as honour bound and battle born as the Bearlings. Rothgore, a young grizzly cub who still stood seven feet tall, was exactly what you would expect from the bear-strand of Beastmen. He looked like a grizzly bear with the brown fur and clawed paws, but he stood upright on legs more developed then his mundane kind. His was a race of proud warriors whose response to an insult was combat.

"I offer before you the same wager I give each new recruit," Venter said with a sly smile. "Prove your worth in our combat ring. If you succeed, you will not have to train in combat, but if you fail, you will attend each class, without fail and without argument until you have seen the difference between a warrior and a Hellguard."

Rothgore was the first to respond, accepting the challenge without a moment's doubt, and a couple more followed. Behind Venter, the eager Hellguards exchanged coins, the wagers, on who would accept the challenge.

"Get some sleep, men," he said with a sly smirk laced with a hint of pity. "For tomorrow you face the gauntlet. Tomorrow you learn what it takes to be a Hellguard."

The world is a vast place and everything within it makes noise. From the beautiful birds soaring in the sky, to the stoic turtles that steadily marches, everything on the planet sends waves of sound across existence, most of these go unheard, or unnoticed, by the average being. But for Quinlan Torn, the man who hears everything, the world is a cascade of torrential noise. As the morning light peered through stained windows and onto his wooden floor, Quinlan sat unmoving at his desk, his ears already ringing by the noise of the world and his eyes eagerly observing every detail of his room.

The world was loud.

Every creak of the floorboards and every scratch of a quill; Quinlan heard it all. Every flicker of sunlight, every speck of dust and every object in the room; Quinlan saw it all. To adapt to the thousands of sounds and millions of sights the human brain had long ago developed a filter. Most people can't recognize or notice the trillions of stimuli that occurs in the world around them, it would drive them insane; but for the man who can, the one who notices everything, the world and its sounds and sights becomes a botched opera, with a muffled orchestra where each instruments blends in with the one beside it and the flicker of lights glow directly into his eyes. For one like Quinlan, there exists no alternative then to shut out the world and live only for him.

Quinlan stood up, dressed in a linen nightgown, and walked across the room to his double door armoire. He opened the wooden doors -- left door, then right -- exactly identical to every other time he opened it. His equipment delicately hung, each from a specific spot that belong to it and no other. His armoire was always the same, always identical. It started with his armour, a studded leather affair, which hung at the far left side. Next to it was his dress uniform, a three-piece suit he rarely wore, then three pairs of slacks, six shirts, and seventeen pairs of socks, each carefully placed in the pull out drawer.

Quinlan quickly dressed, using the same order as every day before. First, he started with the socks, then the pants, followed by the shirt, the belt, his tunic, gloves, and finally his boots. Never had that order changed, nor would it. For one like Quinlan, one who has forsaken the world and its noises and lights, all that was left for the broken man to focus on was him and his surroundings. Quinlan lived by details; everything had its place and nothing could absent. The more he focused on the details of his life, the more inwards Quinlan became.

Satisfied that everything lay where it should, Quinlan exited his room and descended the stairs to the mess hall below. The lower he got, the louder the orchestra became, constantly increasing in volume but never in clarity. Quinlan quietly counted as he descended, designating each step with a vocal number, until he reached the bottom. Five floors down at twenty-five stairs a floor gave his trip one hundred and twenty-five steps in total, and he'd counted them all numerous times.

The mess hall was row after row of tables and their accompanying chairs. Dozens of men, each in their own stage of armoured dress, sat at the tables dining on the first meal of the day. They all drank and fed, laughing and talking as they shoveled potatoes, eggs, and various other meats into their mouths, washing it down with cow's milk and mugs of thick black syrup known only as battle brew. Quinlan crossed the hall, mumbling quietly with a small twitch of his head, and approached a vacant seat, his seat. The kitchen staff knew Quinlan -- everybody knew Quinlan -- but the kitchen staff knew his requirements better than most. Quinlan always sat in the same place, his spot, and he always ate alone. His dishware and utensils were placed with a level of meticulous accuracy normally reserved for religious ceremonies; his fork to the left of the plate, the knife and spoon to the right, and the mug just above.

Quinlan eyed the mug with disdain. The handle, usually angled perfectly to the right, was slightly skewed. His mug wasn't where it should have been, the details were wrong. All he had were the details. Quinlan reached for the mug, his fingers grasping the circumference of the rim, and rotated it upwards, the handle pointing to his makeshift north. Like the dial on a safe, he twisted it around until the handle pointed due south, then back towards up just shy of true north. Quinlan continued to twist the mug, first upwards then back down, each time stopping short of where he stopped before until the mug rested still and its handle pointed to his makeshift east. It was all in the details.

His life was in the details.

The golden sand danced across the ground as Venter escorted the recruits onto the training grounds. The recruits were separated into two groups, those who were resigned to training and those who were ready to fight for their skills.

"What stands before you is your test. This circle will be your battlefield where each of you will face a Hellguard of my choosing. Each of you has shown you have the heart to be here," Venter said. "Now you just have to prove you have the skills."

"So in order to prove ourselves," a knight recruit asked in bewilderment, "we have defeat a full fledge combat trained Hellguard?"

"Defeat Quinlan?" The older warrior chuckled in disbelief. "Oh, by the Living God, no. You just have to survive. Over there is a rack of wooden weapons. Pick the one you want and prepare yourself."

Venter walked off, leaving the recruits terrified and confused, as he entered a small waiting room. Sitting alone, in the center of the room, was Quinlan. Venter never knew how to react to Quinlan, nobody ever did, but they had learned to deal with it. Quinlan would just sit in a room, quiet and waiting, until he was told otherwise. He rarely talked to other people unless he needed something, and in truth, for any normal man he'd be more trouble then he was worth, but Quinlan was far from normal.

"Brother Torn. It is time. We need your sword." Venter handed him a wooden blade, a facsimile reserved for training, and pointed to the field. "The time is now for battle. Just please don't kill them."

As his fingers gripped the wooden blade, Quinlan climbed to his feet. Without a word, he walked out into the battle ring. As his leather boots hit the golden sand, his demeanor changed. He stood taller, his eyes narrowed, and the tilt in his head vanished. As the curious crusader entered the ring, the world's stimuli assaulted his senses: the feel of the hesitant morning breeze, the sound of the senior Hellguard making bets, and the smell of fear and uncertainty emanating from the recruits. The world was loud, but the further into the ring he marched, the quieter the world became.

When Quinlan stepped into battle, he changed. He was no longer that inward soul shutting out the world and its millions of stimuli; instead he embraced it all and in those few short moment where steel met steel, he was unbeatable. For the man who saw everything, battle was nothing but a flurry of information. As the first recruit, a sellsword named Ashad, stepped forward, clutching a wooden longsword, Quinlan saw everything. He saw the beads of sweat trickling down the conscript's brow, the unsure grip with his right hand, and the tilted stance on uneven ground.

Quinlan attacked first, a thrust into Ashad's shoulder that caused his stance to buckle, and struck with a downward blow that slapped the recruit's blade from his hand.

With a final sweeping slice, Quinlan knocked the helpless recruit from his feet and sent him crashing to the ground.

The Hellguards cheered as the recruits stared onwards in horror. In a matter of two heartbeats, Quinlan had taken a skilled sellsword, disarmed him, sent him to the ground and struck him down. The next recruit stepped forward, Ser Cavotta, with a board-and-sword fencing style. The peculiar pugilist absorbed the particulars, noticing the minutiae. Cavotta lacked the improper grip and poor stance of Ashad, but came with a limp, the very slight hint of a hobble.

Quinlan attacked as he stepped forward, his wooden facsimile bouncing off the knight's shield with a hollow thud. He struck again, harder and faster, each strike pushing Cavotta to his limit as he tried to simply block the attack. With each hollow thud, the knight was pushed back, his feet shuffling back as he desperately tried to shift from defense to offense. As each strike bounced off the shield, Quinlan could see the impatience growing. The Hellguard attacked once more, except this time his blade moved slower than normal, dangling an opening before the Knight like bait on a hook. It wasn't an opening Ser Cavotta normally would have taken but as the knight's patience quickly poured out like water from the bottom of a broken bucket, so did reason. Bad ideas seemed like good ones, the hair-length chink in the armour seemed miles wide, and the convenient appearance of a hole in his defense seemed like the miraculous moment needed to turn this fight around. Cavotta saw the opening and used it, clumsily slashing at the peculiar pugilist. Quinlan ducked under the blade, caught the knight by his wrist,

and struck with his sword deep into the knight's await-
ing armpit. The knight howled. Quinlan struck again, his
facsimile striking the Cavotta's weak leg. His leg buckled
and he collapsed to the ground like a broken cart.

More coins passed hands as the Hellguards feverishly
cheered. They never bet on who would win, that was never in doubt; what they wagered on was the length of time
it would take before Quinlan would fell another and they
stumbled away with their tails between their legs. Venter happily clapped his hands together. Every recruit who
emerged from a match with Quinlan took away something different. For some like Ashad it was that their skills
they held dear were not enough to survive, for others like
Ser Cavotta it was that the legions of Hell would prey on a
single weakness. For some like Venter, who fought Quinlan not as a recruit but as a seasoned Hellguard, emerg-
ing from the match gave the veteran a new perspective on
what it would take to win this war.

Rothgore growled inquisitively as Venter waved in
two more recruits, a pair of soldiers from the northern
brigades. The bearling leaned forward and watched. The
soldiers, one armed with a longspear and the other with a
faux thinblade, had seen the dawn of battle and had sur-
vived long enough to see its twilight. They moved together and struck in pairs. Their strategy was drawn directly
from a military manuscript. With long rapid strikes, the
spearmen would keep the Hellguard at a distance, pausing only to allow the fencer to move in and strike. When
their target tried to strike back, the spearmen would resume his assault and force him back.

That was the plan, but it failed to survive the first taste

of battle. Rothgore found himself growling in astonishment as Quinlan held his own. The furless was unlike any Beastmen or any of his own kin. He moved like the wind and seemed to see all that it reached. The Ferocious Furless twisted like a falling leaf as the spearhead harmlessly brushed by him while his wooden facsimile blocked attacks from behind without even looking. He seemed to know when the soldiers were going to attack even before they knew and he always seemed to be able to dodge or block them. He took the strength of numbers the soldiers had and turned it against them, sending partner crashing into partner with but a few twists, turns, and pushes. Before long, the two were tripping over one another, their legs becoming balls of string cursed with knots. The fencer returned to his feet, snapping orders at the spearman as they shifted their tactic and prepared for another assault.

The Bearling let an amused growl grow in the back of his throat. He'd seen the dawn of battle and he'd seen when the first taste of war turned the battle plan sour. This was the test of a soldier, be they beast or man. A good soldier, like the fencer, would adapt, concoct a new plan and try to overcome; a feeble one would sacrifice the plan and fight for themselves. The spearman, climbing back to his feet, had forsaken the plan with an angry shout and charged in. He spun his spear like an eastern bō staff and struck with a flurry of attack. The spearman had speed, at the cost of his full reach, and he tried to use it to overwhelm the furless champion, but as Rothgore watched, amused at soldier's attempt at rage, he could see how Quinlan reacted. He moved quicker than before, spinning less in favour of quick blocks, and allowing the bō to strike his arms and legs all in sacrifice to get close. Even with his thick furry hide for protection, Rothgore could still empathize with each stinging blow of the wooden staff, cringing at the thought of the pain, but Quinlan, much like a berserker, seemed to shrug it off and push forward. Come the end of this battle, he would feel the pain, suffer for his sacrifice, but while the skirmish continued he would barely notice it. Finally close enough to strike, Quinlan struck with his wooden facsimile, snapping at the spearmen's wrist and knee until both buckled.

It happened so quickly that had Rothgore or any other spectator had blinked they would have missed it. The spearman tumbled to the ground, like the Wyrnica towers ten years ago, the wooden sword tossed aside like discarded newborn and the bō staff snatched out of the air like a tossed ball. Quinlan, with the bō in hand and the spearman laying at his feet, turned to face the fencer. Like a windmill of attacks, his staff spun, striking at the lone solider. The fencer blocked what he could, dodged what was possible, and suffered the wrath of the blows that went unanswered. To his credit, the fencer was continuously trying to adapt, shifting his tactics to a more aggressive style, to a faster moving style, and even once taking up Quinlan's discarded sword and duel-wielding, but just like the other he too eventually fell, a close lining swipe neck followed by a powerful downwards slap to his chest.

The spectators leapt over the fence and pulled the two fallen soldiers to safety. Venter could see the looks on their faces as each man realized the new truth they'd taken away from the battle. For the spearmen, no lesson drove home harder than that of teamwork. He needed to gain complete faith in his Hellguard brothers if he dared to survive. For the fencer it was speed, not in his arms or legs, but in his mind. He was quick to adapt, but he acted rashly in doing so. He needed to learn how to see a fight for what it was and quickly breakdown the facts, traits that existed in every battlefield commander. The seed of leadership was buried deep within that fencer; the Hellguard needed only to nourish it and it would grow.

Venter looked back at the last recruit willing to step into the ring. Five had dared to prove their skills and four had fallen. This left only the Bearling; it was Rothgore's time for battle. With a fearsome roar, he marched to the ring, ignoring the weapons as he passed, and leapt over the wooden divider. With a loud thud, his paws landed on the golden sand. He clenched his toes, his claws digging into the amber grains. With a menacing growl, he approached the furless fighter, his fingers beckoning the human to strike.

Quinlan eased the grip on his staff as he started to spin his weapon in circles, slowly at first but quickly gaining speed. The staff was like a serpent, coiled back waiting to strike the moment its desired prey moved within range. The end of the wooden staff shot out like an arrow, slapping against the thick hide before the Bearling even saw it move. Quinlan struck thrice, moving up the body from the torso, to the shoulder and finally aiming at the head. Rothgore winced in pain at the first two strikes, his fur doing little to protect him, but as the bō darted towards his skull, the Bearling reacted. He grabbed the weapon with both hands and gave it a yank. Quinlan, succumbing to Rothgore's great strength, stumbled forward to meet a massive paw grabbing him by the neck and hoisting him into the air. Rothgore, clutching the man with a choke-hold, sneered as he held the pink skin a foot above the earth. With a roar of delight, he slammed the man on the ground and kicked him squarely in the chest, the power-ful Bearling blow sending the pink skin skipping across the sand like a stone to water.

The Hellguard's roars of glee mimicked the Bearling's frightening battle cry. They had not seen a battle the likes of this in eons. In his younger days, Rothgore would have cheered and gloated, but he'd seen battles where creatures beaten to a hair's length of their life got back to their feet and continued fighting. The Bearling knew that if any-body could come back after a devastating slam, it would be this human.

"Rise, human," Rothgore called out. He pitched the bō staff across the ring and roared once more. "If we fight, we do so without weapons. We fight with fist and paw alone. Now face me!"

Quinlan's body cried for reprieve. The throbbing was great and he had a sneaking suspicion that one or two of his ribs had cracked, but the pain was meaningless. He climbed to his feet and slowly marched back at the bear. A normal man would be scared or mad after a devastating blow, but fate had long since forsaken normality for Quin-lan. He wasn't angry or pissed, and he wasn't succumbing to fear or pride; his face was a blank canvas, untouched by the painter. Quinlan face was void of emotion. With each step the human took, the quieter the world became. He absorbed every minute stimuli of the world: the smell of the air, the taste of the wind, the way the bear stood on the golden sand. Quinlan noticed the twitch of Rothgore's muscles, the squint in his eyes, and the way his lips quivered as he tried to hold back his rage.

When he was a merely a few feet away, Quinlan burst into a sprint. His foot struck out and slammed out into Rothgore's left knee. The leg buckled and the bear dropped to one knee. The human belted the bear's neck with his elbow and spun with a devastating right crossover punch, a combination that could have downed a regular man, but did little but stun the beastman. With each punch the world got quieter, the normally deafening noise of life fading until there was only silence, until all that he could hear was his own laboured breathing. This was the moment of pure clarity, when the secrets of the world became as clear as words on a page. Sand pushed to the right meant an incoming kick, a twitch in the arm illustrated a furious swipe, and the direction of the wind gave him a heartbeat more time to dodge a punch. The two warriors fought, Quinlan striking with a flurry of precise shots while Rothgore unleashed his unending fury. As his rage grew, so did his speed and strength. Quinlan had been trying to avoid every blow possible, for even a block left his arm numb, but now, with Rothgore's hate pushing his strength of un-human levels, every hit was ruinous and the bear was just getting faster. Like the orange flame of the sun, Rothgore never seemed to tire -- he just burned brighter.

Every punch Quinlan fired into the bear's hide was like punching a furry wall, thick and resilient, but even the massive stonewalls that protected the Enclave city would crumble if struck enough. Rothgore was beginning to crumble. His step wavered, his arm seemed heavy and limp, and the spring in his step seemed to have snapped. Rothgore lunged, wrapping his massive arms around the human and tightly squeezed. The Bearling knew he couldn't last much longer, but neither could the human. He needed to end this now. Quinlan squirmed as he tried to free himself, the wavering beast's strength still more than enough to crush him. Try as he might, his body was firmly secured save for his right arm. Pulling it free, Quinlan slammed it into the bear's chin. It wasn't a powerful punch, there was no strength left in either of them for power, but what he lacked in force he gained in accuracy; at this range he couldn't miss. Over and over he punched the bear's face until both it, and Quinlan's fist, were stained with blood. The pair collapse to the sand as Rothgore's body suddenly went limp. The test between the fist and the grapple was over. Quinlan had held out against unconsciousness. Quinlan had won the match, but only barely.

Then the noise returned.

Venter calling a halt, the rush of cleric and priest, the chanting of healing incantations, and the cheering of Hellguard veterans and recruits alike; like a tornado it came without warning, assaulting his senses like the poor farmer whose crops and livestock are destroyed by the act of the Living God. The pain he'd ignored cried out, furious that it had been paid no heed, but Quinlan didn't make a scream. He just winced and mumbled quietly to himself.

"This was never about your skills," Venter explained to the recruits. "Skills can be taught and perfected. What you needed to witness, especially those of you who have seen battle, is that we are not fighting men nor elves or even the beast races. We are fighting evil itself. One day we will push the legions of hell back, we will stuff them back into the hole they climbed out of, and we will shut the door behind them. Each of you needed to see what it was going to take to do just that."

Venter looked back at Quinlan. A battle with him was like a battle with one's self. You step into the ring thinking you're there for a duel and step out like you would a classroom. You always learned something. Even Venter Zug, who had witnessed the horrors of the hellish onslaught firsthand, left the ring with a newfound clarity. He looked over at Rothgore. The Bearling pushed away the healers as he looked at his paws in disbelief. His face was the same as Venter's had been all those years ago. Both of them had taken the same lesson from Quinlan. Both had suddenly realised what it what it was going to take to be a Hellguard, to win this war.

Victory would require nothing less than the unwavering dedication at all cost.

When evils of hell march unopposed,
And the heart of man was left exposed.
From above blood rain fell from the sky,
When not even the larks would bravely fly
On that field stood only brave men,
Who fought and died time and again.
All that was left on an earth so scarred
Were the men and women of the Hellguard.

Christopher Walsh

Christopher Walsh is an author from Brigus South, Newfoundland. "Stealing Back Freedom" is a prequel story from his fantasy series *Gold & Steel*.

Since 2012, Chris has been crafting the massive world of Gold & Steel and putting together what would be his first entries into the even bigger world of publishing: *As Fierce as Steel* and *Stealing Back Freedom*.

When not writing, Chris works as an apprentice carpenter and enjoys reading a variety of material with particular interest in other fantasy works. He's also an avid video gamer and hiker.

Stealing Back Freedom

They were three, left alone in a darkened woodshed to wait. Orangecloak had always liked the smell of freshly sawn birch. It had a calming effect on her that was most welcome in such stressful times.

Although, there was at least one among them didn't find it so soothing. "Myles, for the love of all things, sit. You're going to wear a hole in the damn floor," she said to her friend. He had been pacing since the scouts had gone out, working himself into a ball of nerves like he always did.

He chose to remain standing, but at least came to a stop before the row of wood Orangecloak had commandeered as a seat. "I saw a lot of guards when we snuck into town, Orangecloak. I think you should call off the protest for the day," he stated, as she knew he would. Myles was cautious by nature and protective of Orangecloak at the best of times.

From beside her stirred Coquarro, her other constant companion. "It's Aquas Bay, Myles. We're in the home of Illiastra's naval fleet. There's always a heavy presence of guards. I tell you this every time. Red asked you to sit and I agree with her. Spinning in circles isn't going to improve our situation," Coquarro told Myles. Red was the only name that Coquarro had ever known Orangecloak by, going back to the day they had met on the island refuge of Phaleayna all those years ago. One of his thick, callused dark hands found its way onto her knee. "Have you thought about what you're going to say today?"

"Something similar to what I usually say, I think," Orangecloak answered with a shrug. "I haven't given it much thought."

Myles wagged a finger at her. "You're too lackadaisical, Orangecloak. You should have your speech ready in the back of your head. We won't have much time for a protest today, and every second you waste trying to think of things to say on the spot is time the guards will use to move in on you."

"Calm down, Myles," Coquarro said with a shake of his head.

"No, I won't calm down, Coquarro," Myles responded, trying hard to keep his frustration from getting the better of him. "You heard what people are saying: There's a ship from Daol Bay docked in port from Lord Tullivan's own fleet and the Master of Blades himself was seen disembarking from it. He's here, Coquarro and if he knows Orangecloak is too, he's going to come after her. Who's going to stop him? Are you naïve enough to think you can fight off Tryst Reine? I know I can't."

In truth, the news had been weighing on Orangecloak's mind as much as it had Myles', but she was Field Commander of the Thieves; whatever worries burdened her, she could not show them. "We don't know that it will come to that, Myles. It's a fairly large city; the Master of Blades might be anywhere within its walls. If our scouts see him in the market, where we are to protest, then we will call it off."

Myles remained unconvinced. "I still don't think it right that we go through with it, Orangecloak. If the Master of Blades is in town, then that means that Lord Master Grenjin Howland might be here as well and he travels with the Honourable Guardsmen about him."

"If the Lord Master of Illiastra were on that ship, people would be talking more about that than they would the Master of Blades, Myles," Orangecloak pointed out. "It would seem that Tryst Reine came alone. He's probably here for a vacation. In fact, I bet he's on his way to the Red Isles for some rest and relaxation as we speak."

"What if he's not?" Myles offered as a counterpoint. "By the gods, what if he knew you were coming here and was sent alone to do the deed of killing you himself? We should be on our way out of the city and heading for the ruins of Amarosha right now before he has his chance to do anything, Orangecloak."

Coquarro groaned and leaned forward from the high row of wood he had been using as a backrest. "For goodness sake, Myles, do you even hear yourself? We've been in Aquas Bay half a hundred times doing this very thing and you've never been craven before. It's not going to be any different now. The Master of Blades is just one man in a city of tens of thousands."

That drew a scoff from Myles and he threw his hands up. "Tryst Reine is the *Master of Blades*," he argued, putting heavy emphasis on those two words above all. "He is the best swordsman in the known world, the sworn protector of the Lord Master and given to serve with full authority and full immunity from all laws. That man can do whatever he so pleases in the name of the Lord Master, and Orangecloak is the most wanted person in all of Illiastra. Do you think it coincidence that they're in the same city together? I'm telling you both, he knows she is here and he has come to make the arrest."

Despite knowing how stubborn Myles could be, Orangecloak knew she must try to reason with him. "They call Tryst Reine the Master of Blades, but that is a title only earned by students of the University of Combative Arts in the nation of Drake. How many have there been that were called Master of Blades? Only two or three in a thousand years, right? We all know who the first Master of Blades was: Segai, the Great Hero of Phaleayna. We've seen his bones and the remnants of his plate armour in the crypts behind Great Valley Lake. I don't think you can earn the name Master of Blades if you don't somehow embody his heroic traits. Besides, this Tryst Reine is a sell sword. He's sworn no oaths, said no vows, and his loyalty to the Lord Master is made of paper. I doubt he spends his days worrying about pleasing Grenjin Howland. Also, consider that if he was all he's made out to be and he wanted to find us, it would not have taken him four years to do so."

"Red speaks sense, Myles," Coquarro said in an attempt to assuage Myles' concerns. "If she is not worried, then you should not be either."

It did worry Orangecloak, though. Not that she could say as much, but the notion that Tryst Reine was in the city was one she found troubling. If what she had heard about him out of Atrebell, Illiastra's capital, bore any truth, then he was a monster, as morally depraved as he was skilled with a sword. Oftentimes, stories that made their way across the Varras River and into the Southlands had a way of becoming exaggerated along the way, but Orangecloak could not dismiss them outright. Some among her ranks believed the tales of Tryst Reine to be mere fabrications, knowing that the Lord Master and his Elite Merchant Party frequently spread such lies; all of it done to bolster fear in the populace of Illiastra toward their government. Fear that Orangecloak and their Thieves worked tirelessly to dispel.

If nothing else, it will not do to let these tales cloud my perception. It is on me to rise above the fear mongering of the EMP, I cannot let myself be swayed by it, Orangecloak told herself, as she often did.

At the very least, her words had sated Myles enough to make him stop pacing. Though steady, he was still anxious and fidgeting and he idly picked a bit of sawdust that had fallen into Orangecloak's long red hair that tumbled well past her shoulders. For a moment Myles looked as though he was going to break his brief silence, but just as he opened his mouth, a scarcely audible knock came on the door.

There was not as much as a breath while the three of them waited. Coquarro raised a hand with three fingers raised and counted them down wordlessly until he was at a fist. The person without knocked again, this time in a pattern of rap-a-tap-rap-a-tap tap-tap-tap, repeating it over again twice more.

Myles exhaled with relief and went to the old door,

peeking through a knothole in the wood for added security before finally unlatching it. "It's Ellarie and her ladies," he declared as he stepped back, door in hand and gave entry to four cloaked figures, hoods drawn and heads down.

Only when Myles closed the door behind them did the four reveal their faces. They were young and fair, near Orangecloak's age but all younger by a few years, save for one.

"You're the first to return, Ellarie," Orangecloak told her first lieutenant and dear friend. "Have you crossed paths with the other lieutenants?"

Ellarie shook out the dark, wavy hair that fell just past her ears before she answered. "I haven't seen Merion, Joyce, or Lazlo since we split up this morning. I just came across Edwin and Garlan not far from here. They were coming to report that they had spotted the Master of Blades. When we found one another, they gave their report to me and returned from whence they came to keep an eye on him."

"Well, where was he? What was he doing?" Myles asked eagerly.

"He was in the market square," Ellarie began to answer.

"See, Orangecloak?" Myles said, rudely cutting Ellarie off. "I told you that's where he'd be, he knows you're coming-"

Ellarie returned the gesture and stepped in. "The Master of Blades was buying an expensive bottle of liquor. He left the market as soon as he had it and seemed content to wile his morning away in a small inn several streets away, drinking mead and eating mutton in the common room."

"See, Myles?" Orangecloak mimicked him jokingly. "I told you that you were working yourself up over nothing. I think you owe Ellarie an apology."

He grumbled and turned to the first lieutenant of the Thieves. "Sorry, El, I shouldn't have cut you off like that. Still though, we should keep Edwin and Garlan in position to track Tryst Reine, if he's still at the inn."

With an overdue stretch, Orangecloak slid from the woodpile to stand up. "Indeed, Myles. I intend for Edwin and Garlan to stay on him. What of your own scouting trip, Ellarie?"

"Outside of the Master of Blades' presence, there's nothing unusual to report," Ellarie went on. "This is Breakday, so the markets are bustling and you should have a large audience. We counted six guards and one overseer patrolling inside the market, all armed with swords and pistols and in groups of two." She gestured towards a fellow raven-haired woman standing beside her and to one of the two blondes. "Bernadine and Nia were sent to the rooftops and they counted just two riflemen stationed up there today. I think standard procedure should be enough to distract them all without incident."

Orangecloak considered everything she heard and looked to the last blonde. "What about you, Coramae? This is your hometown. Did you see anything out of the ordinary?"

The woman had been looking all around the shed and looked surprised to hear her name. "No, milady, I noticed nothing worth reporting."

"That settles it, then," Orangecloak decided. "Once Lazlo, Merion, and Joyce return, we will proceed." She eyed Coramae again, still glancing all about the tiny building. "Coramae, we will likely have time before everyone else arrives; if you'd like, you can go have a look around your old house."

"I think I would like that, milady, thank you," Coramae said.

Orangecloak gave her a nod. "Take Nia with you and keep an eye out for the others. Return to the shed if you see them."

The two departed and Myles latched the door behind them once again.

"That poor thing, I feel for her," Coquarro said from where he still sat on the woodpile. "It's been two years since she and her friend Alia came to us and she's still so full of longing."

"I feel badly every time we drag either of them back here," Ellarie commented sadly. "This was their home, I know, and they know this city better than anyone, but they've been through so much here."

Orangecloak pitied Coramae and her friend as much as anyone. "It was the EMP that was responsible for what happened to them. They came for Allia's father's tailoring business, tore down his building and give him a pittance for it. As if that wasn't enough, they drafted her oldest brother into the Illiastran armed forces and arrested her father when he complained about the whole thing. He's in Biddenhurst now, as is her mother. We all know that anyone who goes to the Prison City never returns."

"You forget that Coramae's family fared just as poorly after she left," Ellarie reminded her. "Her father died at sea and her mother was not permitted to earn a wage under the laws of the Triarchy religion. Coramae doesn't even know what happened to her, or her younger siblings for that matter. Biddenhurst again, I would imagine. Although, her siblings might be holed up in a Triarchy orphanage somewhere. Though, I don't think that's necessarily any better."

Bernadine stepped forward. "With all due respect to the both of you, I don't know one of us that *haven't* come to the Thieves through tragic circumstances." Though she was the youngest of Ellarie's unit, Bernadine was wise beyond her years, unwaveringly loyal and perpetually sullen and stoic.

"That's a fair point, Bernadine," Orangecloak agreed.

From the corner of her eye, Orangecloak espied Myles taking a sudden peek through the knothole again. "Someone's coming, looks like Lazlo and he's alone."

As Ellarie before him had done, Lazlo knocked, waited and went about tapping out the same pattern three times over. He was admitted and the instant Myles closed the door behind him he had his cloak drawn back, sending long, blonde ringlets tumbling over his toned shoulders. "By Aren's beard, it's too bloody hot outside for wearing cloaks," Lazlo said to no one in particular as he wiped at the beads of sweat forming on his forehead with his cloak.

That garnered an amused scoff from Coquarro. "You know nothing of heat, my friend. Remind me to take you to Johnah someday. The desert in the interior of my country will make you beg for the ocean breezes of Aquas Bay in summer."

"Forgive me if I somehow forget to take you up on that offer, Coquarro," Lazlo said with a jovial wink to the tall, dark skinned man before turning his attention to Orange-cloak. "Donnis, Etcher and I had quite the busy morning, despite the unyielding heat and humidity."

"Speaking of those two, where are they?" Ellarie asked quickly. "Also, did you happen to come across my sister and Joyce?"

Lazlo produced a canteen hanging from a leather thong around his neck and took a seat beside Coquarro before granting an answer. "Merion, Joyce and the three with them are not far behind, actually. We spaced out our arrivals to avoid suspicion. As for my own lads, I left them to investigate a potential distraction for you on the water-front."

The mere mention of one of Lazlo's distractions caused Orangecloak's brows to furrow. "What sort of damage is this going to cause?" she asked suspiciously.

"Just some bruises, broken noses and busted lips on a bunch of sailors," Lazlo explained with a sly grin. "There's a ship in port from one of the nations from the Crescent Is-land's, Gallick, to be exact and this particular ship of Gal-licians are looking particularly surly today. Donnis and Etcher were just going to instigate a little scuffle between them and the crew of a merchant ship from Weicaster Bay docked nearby. Both crews are drinking heartily as we speak, so it wouldn't take much to set the Gallicians on them, but it would require quite the compliment of guards to get in between the brawl."

"Your damn distractions are always more trouble than they're worth," Orangecloak said with a shake of her head, though she didn't dismiss it outright. "Keep Donnis and Etcher there, but don't do anything unless we absolutely have to. It might be that our usual tactics will suffice to draw the guards out of the marketplace." She passed a hand through her red locks and sighed loudly. "At any rate, go on with your report."

Lazlo casually crossed his legs and took another sip of water. "Right then, you may be interested to hear that the Master of Blades doesn't seem to be in Aquas Bay for any official reason. It's purely pleasure… A lot of pleasure, if I do say so."

She narrowed her gaze on him. "How did you come into this information?"

"There's a certain city councillor's assistant who is willing to tell me everything he might hear just to keep me coming back to his bed," Lazlo admitted with tongue in cheek. "Although it may also be to prevent me from telling his wife and the rest of the world that he enjoys *having* me in his bed. Either way, I sought him out and he told me that Tryst hasn't been to visit Minister Polliane or any of his city councillors nor anyone else related to the EMP. However, our sellsword friend has been spending a great deal of time going between a cheap inn and an expensive brothel since arriving in the city."

Orangecloak thought that a little puzzling. "The protector and enforcer of the very same Lord Master that views prostitution as a crime worthy of public flogging and lifetime imprisonment has been seen frequenting a brothel? Are you certain of this?"

"Quite," Lazlo told her, his smug grin never fading. "As it is, I happen to know one of the workers there, so I did a little more digging around. Apparently, he's been spending all his nights with a freckled, brunette woman near our age named Sinzia."

"So he came to Aquas Bay to drink and #&@%," Coquarro concluded with what they were all thinking. "Not exactly my idea of scandalous. However, the good news is that he should not be a problem for us. Is there anything else you have to add, Lazlo?"

Lazlo clicked his teeth while he thought about it before ultimately giving a quick shake of his head. "That's all I've got. The other Dollen sister and Joyce went deep into the market with the other Aquas Bay girl. They'll have a better report."

All eyes were on Orangecloak then, waiting on her order. She dusted off her green leather trousers, matching bodice, and white, sleeveless tunic and took a deep breath. "We're going ahead as planned. I'll meet Joyce and Merion on the road to the market and give them their orders. Coquarro and Myles, as always, are with me. Ellarie, separate your unit into pairs as you see fit, harry the ground patrols and lead them out of the market. Lazlo, ready your men on their distraction. If I feel we need the extra help, I'll have Myles give you a signal before I start the rally. I'll stand in the market as long as I can and when the time comes I'll make my escape by rooftop. We'll meet outside the town walls in the south woods gathering point after it's all over. If you're not there by nightfall, we'll move on to the Amarosha ruins and you can find us there. Does anyone have any questions?"

When no one spoke up, Orangecloak took that as an affirmation and extended a fist, finding it soon joined in a circle with the others, everyone touching knuckle to knuckle.

"We are the Thieves," Orangecloak stated in a strong, firm voice.

They looked to her and answered as one with the three words that had come to be a mantra and rallying cry alike for their movement: "Stealing back freedom."

As they had arrived, so too did they leave: Ellarie and Bernadine went first, to collect Nia and Coramae and make for the market. After a few minutes had passed, Lazlo departed with Myles, so that they could work out a means of sending signal from the marketplace to the waterfront. Once they left, Coquarro latched the door behind them, leaving him and Orangecloak alone to wait and leave last.

He came to stand before her, his big hands on her shoulders. "Are you ready, Red?"

"As much as I ever will be," she answered firmly while reaching into the pocket of her trousers and drawing out a green ribbon to tie back her red hair into a neat tail.

Coquarro knelt and scooped up the weighty satchel that had been between his feet where he sat and slung it across a shoulder. From within he drew a brown, linen cloak and handed it over. "I have your other one tied in a neat little bundle and at the ready."

"Good," she said with a nod as she fastened the light cloak about her shoulders and drew the deep hood down to cover her face. "Let's be off."

"And may good fortune be upon us," Coquarro added as he brought his own hood up.

Outside the air was sultry hot and Orangecloak sympathised with Lazlo's disdain at wearing a cloak at all, even if it was made of linen. She and Coquarro walked side by side down a dirt road, passing a few other farmsteads. There were but a few in this one corner of the city that were permitted to keep small patches of land for livestock and produce, nestled safely beneath the walls. The family of Coramae had been one such farmstead, though when the family fell from grace, their home and land had been forfeited to the EMP. Their house and shed sat empty, waiting to be razed so the land could be sold off.

Green knolls and quaint homes soon gave way to crowded houses that were lumped together and fronting on streets bustling with activity. People passed, shoulders were bumped, but no heed was paid to the pair of cloaked strangers. As long as her face and trademark hair were covered, Orangecloak could get about fairly easily in any city. Even then, passage wasn't impossible, provided she wasn't wearing the brightly coloured cloak her name derived from.

A couple were walking in the street ahead of Orangecloak and Coquarro. The man wore a grey, velvet suit and matching wide brimmed hat and the woman was in a light blue dress and white bonnet. Their pace was tediously slow and Orangecloak nudged Coquarro to make a move to walk around them.

"There you are. I was starting to think you had second thoughts on this whole operation," the woman suddenly said to Orangecloak as they began to walk around them.

Orangecloak looked into her face to find Merion Dollen, sister of Ellarie, staring back. The younger Dollen was light complexioned and freckled like Orangecloak, with her own head of red hair falling in long, natural curls. Given those similarities and the fact that they were of near the same height and size, Merion had taken on the role of being Orangecloak's double. Whenever a protest was staged, Merion was there and dressed in raiment to match Orangecloak to serve as a diversion during the inevitable fleeing.

She eyeballed Merion and Joyce beside her, dressed in the suit. "Where did you two get these getups?" Orangecloak inquired whimsically.

Merion shrugged nonchalantly. "An untended clothesline behind a large house is a great place to find a new wardrobe."

"You know I don't approve of that," Orangecloak reminded Merion with a hard stare. "We may be known as the Thieves, but we do not steal from the people."

Joyce Keena, the lean muscled, hard hitting, blonde haired lover of Merion leaned out around Merion's bonnet to get a glimpse of Orangecloak. "The people we took these clothes from will not miss them," she argued while rolling her shoulders and looking herself over. "Look at this suit; the man who can afford this is not in a sore need for coin."

There was little time to squabble over it and Orangecloak reluctantly pushed beyond the issue to more pressing matters. "I assume you're both wearing your own clothes beneath those outfits. We're going ahead with the plan. You might have been told by the others already: Tryst Reine is not going to be an issue for us. Where is your unit?"

"Aye, my sister came through here and told us everything," Merion replied, her voice dropping to her usual, serious tone. "I left Ami and Alia in the market with a plan to draw away the riflemen on the rooftops. Barring something unforeseen cropping up, your path should be cleared by the time you need to flee."

All while they talked, the four kept moving towards their destination. Directly ahead lay a crossroads between the poorer neighbourhood they were leaving and the more upscale homes and businesses of the upper reaches of the middle class. The streets were wider, but no less crowded, and the four turned off the main road and into a dusty alley. Orangecloak's two lieutenants ducked into a tiny, covered alcove and immediately began undressing.

With the bonnet yanked off, Merion made a single, deft move and pulled the dress over her head. Beneath was a full outfit nearly identical to Orangecloak's, right down to her worn and weathered leather boots.

"You've done great work, as usual," Orangecloak complimented them. "Merion, I want you in place on the roof of the naval recruitment building. Hide behind the spire and wait for me." She turned her attention to Joyce, who was down to her smallclothes and digging her own gear from a satchel that had been stashed in a crate. "When the guard's reinforcements arrive, I'm going to head towards the waterfront. Myles and Coquarro will be with me and we'll leave town near the lighthouse tower in the southwest corner of town. I'm leaving it to you to ensure that everyone else gets out. We'll convene at the Stone Horn in the south woods."

Joyce gave Orangecloak a confident wink while pulling a faded, short-sleeved tunic over her head and topping it with a padded leather vest. "You can count on me," Joyce assured Orangecloak as she cinched her vest tight with a matching leather belt. "I'll be sure to get all of ours out safely before evening."

Orangecloak glanced about the alley to ensure they were alone. "I have faith in you," she said, while extending a fist towards her lieutenants. "We are the Thieves."

"Stealing back freedom," they answered, touching her knuckles with their own.

That's where she left them, fastening old, faded cloaks into place and doing final inventory checks.

For her and Coquarro, it was time to go into the heart of the city and tug at its strings.

Aquas Bay was not a spacious city, by any means, but it was densely populated. The thick, stone walls that protected the denizens from the roving gangs of raiders that lay beyond had made expansion of the city limits impossible. As a result, it seemed as though everyone in the Southlands that had emigrated to the protective embrace of Aquas Bay had just piled in on top of one another. Nowhere was that more evident than in the tightly packed neighbourhoods surrounding the marketplace. Here, it was teeming with people at all hours of the day. These were the working poor, mostly and those even less fortunate than they.

It was easy for Orangecloak to blend in here, so long as she kept her head down. These were the citizens she worked to endear herself to, and her work all around Illiastra had yielded her celebrity and empathy from many. Though few among the populace dared to vocalise their support for the Thieves, Orangecloak could see who her sympathisers were when they recognised her face. Some nodded in silent understanding, while others just stared, with hope and anxiousness in their eyes. They would not alert the guards or impede her passage, but rather they would wait and see if she would speak.

If there were eyes on her this day, Orangecloak could not see them through the sea of humanity before her. The closer she and Coquarro came to the market, the closer the crowds were pressed. Soon they were beneath the archway built between two shops that stood as the entrance to the market, with neither sympathiser nor detractor aware that Lady Orangecloak was among them. Her eyes fell to the wrought iron lettering dangling from the red brick arching span: A Free Market for a Free People.

Except it never was free, was it? Orangecloak thought to herself. *The Elite Merchants peddle in that illusion while holding the reins in their own greedy hands.*

Another woman in a hooded cloak sidled up beside the pair and looked directly at Orangecloak. "My girls are in position," Ellarie told her in a voice that was equal parts nervousness and excitement. "Are you ready?"

"I am ready, aye," Orangecloak answered. "Joyce, Ami, and Alia are due on the roofs any moment to lead the riflemen away. That's your cue."

Ellarie gave Orangecloak a nod and disappeared back into the masses once more.

Inside the market the air somehow seemed stuffier and it was stiflingly hot. Orangecloak scanned the rooftops, looking for the three women or Myles and finding neither of them.

Coquarro leaned down to her ear level. "Shall we go

for the merchant's stall in front of Benson's Jewels again?" he asked.

"Aye, it's the best location," Orangecloak replied while still looking about worriedly. "I don't see any of ours up above yet."

"They will come, Red," he assured her. "Joyce was still readying herself when we left her. Give her a little more time."

She knew Coquarro was right, yet she remained nervous all the same. In the four years since Orangecloak's appointment to the title of Field Commander, her Thieves had grown quite efficient at planning and executing these demonstrations. There had been many before and usually her group came away unscathed. Though without fail, her stomach fluttered and a dark thought crept forward from the recesses of her mind. Each time the Thieves succeeded the thought grew louder until it practically screamed at her. *Have I pressed my luck too far? Is this the day it all comes apart at the seams and I fall from grace? So what if it is? The wheels are in motion and I can go no way but forward.*

If this is it, let them say I went out fighting.
If this is it, may the dream live on after me.
If this is it…

"We're here."

Orangecloak looked around to find that she and Coquarro were huddled between two stacks of crates beside a whitewashed brick wall and he was staring at her curiously. "Now is not the time for the mind to wander. Prepare yourself, for your moment is at hand."

Despite the doubt plaguing her, Orangecloak managed to give Coquarro a smile that she hoped displayed some measure of confidence. "Don't worry, Coquarro, I am. I was merely going over my speech to myself," she lied. "Could you go and check the skyline and let me know when Joyce and the others have begun their distractions?"

He gave her a wink and half of a smile of his own. "Of course, Red, I'd be glad to."

Once he had gone back into the fray, Orangecloak pulled her hood tighter, crouched low and took a pair of long, deep breaths to clear her mind. She heard men shouting and a collective gasp from the crowd and shortly after it Coquarro's voice, drawing her back once more. "It is done. Joyce and her pair of Thieves have sprung and Ellarie's crew have drawn the ground patrols away." He squeezed around her, put his back to the wall and cupped his hands at waist level. "Go now, so that their effort is not in vain."

"Aye, I'm ready," she said, finding her will in that instant. Her right hand went to the clasp of the brown cloak and it fell away to the ground. Repeating a move practiced a hundred times before, Orangecloak set a foot into Coquarro's hands and his strong arms vaulted her upward. As the lip of the roof of the stall came into sight, she grabbed it and clung tightly with her fingertips, feet scrabbling for purchase in the mortar lines of the bricks. With a last push she was up and looking over the whole market.

From here she could see almost the entire square laid out before her. It gave her a good vantage point of the main access points, though she was not so high up that she could not be heard. Her eyes fell to Coquarro, himself opening his satchel to retrieve a bundle that he threw to her above. It was snagged from the air deftly, her hands working quickly to untie the brown twine that bound the treasured garment that was her namesake.

It was a cloak that once had been orange but in time had faded to the colour of a peach. As she flung it across her shoulders and clasped it into place, Orangecloak could nearly feel the eyes of the crowd beginning to fall on her. There were whispers and even more heads turning away from the ruckus the other Thieves had incited to the woman standing high above them. *One more thing,* she remembered while reaching for the ribbon that held her ponytail, pulling it loose to let her red hair tumble across her shoulders. *Whoever hasn't noticed my presence before, most certainly will now.*

Orangecloak looked across the market and at the faces before her, raised a hand high and inhaled. "We live in a nation controlled by men who rule over us with fear," she started, speaking in a loud, powerful voice. "These men would make us believe that they are a single, unified entity bigger than any one single person and that we are each alone against them. They send out papers and criers to convince us that we can do nothing to touch them and that we survive because they allow it." She paused, looked about and made eye contact with as many as she could in that moment and spoke again. "I come before you today to tell you that is a lie."

All had turned to face her by then, poor and wealthy alike until a silence had fallen over the entire market. Far to her right, Orangecloak noticed a man in a dapper suit leaning on the railing of a second floor balcony that belonged to a bank. He was joined by others shortly after, one of which she knew to be a city councillor. Even they, the very people she opposed, stared at her in silent anticipation, waiting to hear what she might say.

She began to pace atop the roof in slow, deliberate steps. "When I look at all the men, women, and children before me, I see thousands of faces staring back, all standing side by side, together, if but for a moment. There are more people before me now than all the lords, ministers and councillors in the Elite Merchant Party together."

A man near the front who looked to be but a few years Orangecloak's senior laughed at that statement. "They have an army!" he shouted at her.

"An army comprised of your brothers, fathers, and neighbours," Orangecloak countered without missing a step. "The EMP arrives at your doors to force your own into their ranks, they give them a wage and tell them to do their bidding or rot in Biddenhurst. However, for their own worth, the EMP is but sixty men called lord and minister with five city councillors each for a total of three hundred and sixty. That's all, just three hundred and sixty flesh and blood men, no better than you or I. Just scared, frightened, little men hiding behind an army made of your own to protect themselves from you."

From over the whispering waves of the crowd, she could hear town guards yelling orders to the crowd and to one another to move aside. Out of the corner of her eye, she caught something glinting in the sunlight and looked to the rooftops to her left to see a shape she knew to be Myles. He was using a little mirror to send a signal to Lazlo to spur the brawl on the waterfront. Orangecloak knew that she was growing short of time and went on hurriedly.

"Yet, those few control almost all the wealth and resources of our country and grow fat and wealthy from our labours," she went on to explain to the crowd. "What do we, the many, get for making them, the few, into the controlling hoarders that they are? We are left to survive on the scraps and given the 'right' to serve our overlords. That's it: A mere existence, expectations of servitude and overwhelming fear. That is all we are granted under our current government. The only hope the EMP leaves to the people is that we might die before we are sent off to the prison city to be made slaves of."

There was murmuring from the crowd by now. From the voices closest to her, Orangecloak could hear supporters and detractors alike. The guards had backed off, likely to attend to the melee Lazlo's crew had started, though a few individuals remained, weaving their way through the crowd toward her.

Orangecloak spread her arms wide, in open embrace. "There is a hope, though, however small it may be. It is a hope shared by those like me and the Thieves. Do any among you know what that hope is?"

A woman's voice somewhere to Orangecloak's left spoke up above the others: "You hope that a pox will sweep through the EMP?"

"Do you hope for a quick death when they catch you?" a man japed right before Orangecloak's very feet to a chorus of laughter from other sceptics.

"You hope that we will somehow fear a band of lawless brigands?" roared a voice far to the left and she turned her head to see the same city councillor. His fists tightly gripped the wrought iron railing of the balcony and he leaned out over it.

As she was about to answer, Orangecloak spotted a man standing on the street directly in the line of sight between her and the bank's balcony. Their eyes locked and she froze where she stood. Despite the scorching heat, the man was clad head to heel in black clothing, with a long mane of straight, fiery red hair that touched his waist.

Even dressed as he is, with that head of hair I still might doubt who he was if not for those eyes, Orangecloak thought to herself.

They were a strikingly bright shade of green that she could discern despite the distance. Eyes of that shade were a rare feature and unique to a select few people from the faraway continent of Gildriad. As rare as it was among the three nations of Gildriad, to see someone with the 'Gildraddi Greens' in Illiastra was a rarity above measure and it left no doubt. *Somehow, I knew you would come, Master of Blades,* Orangecloak thought. *I tried to convince myself otherwise, but I knew you would not stay away. If this is it and you are here for me, then may you hear what I have to say, Tryst Reine.*

Orangecloak steeled her resolve, cleared her throat and answered the calls. "Our hope, our tiny, meagre little ray of hope, is that you will learn what the Thieves have all come to know: That power is but nothing but an illusion. The men we give power to are people just as ordinary as you and I, no more worthy of reverence and submission than any other. It is not we who should fear this minority of mere mortals. It is they who should fear a wakened, unified people."

There was a smattering of applause and roaring from the gathered mass, however it was clear that most were still mistrustful, apathetic, or even outright dismissive of her message.

Orangecloak tried to keep her attention on the nearing guards, though her eyes seemed intent on wandering back to the Master of Blades. He was still as stone, arms folded and staring back. On his hip he wore a sword in a red, leather scabbard and Orangecloak knew it must be that fearsome sword made of dwarven blacksteel he was said to wield. Yet, it sat as still as he.

Have my words compelled him to stay his blade? she wondered briefly, before the councillor above him bellowed out once more.

"As you can see, no man here with any good sense will pay heed to raving woman who does not know her place," the councillor roared above the growing noise of the crowd. "You and your kind are naught but verminous, godless outlaws worthy of only continual scorn, a noose for your necks, and the eternal damnation that awaits you."

The soldiers were close enough that Orangecloak could make out brass buttons on the blue jackets of their uniforms. She turned one last time to the councillor, looking between him and the still unmoving Master of Blades below. "No, Councillor, we are none of those things. We are exactly what your party named us all those years ago."

A gloved hand reached for her ankle and Orangecloak kicked it away. She backed towards the wall of the jewellery store and looked to the roof to find Coquarro already there and waiting. He knelt and extended a hand, and Orangecloak darted up the wall to him. She grabbed at the ruts in the mortar and any outcropping bricks she could until she could make a lunge for Coquarro's outstretched arm. In a single, strong lift she was carried to the relative safety of the upper rooftop, where she turned and faced the awestruck crowd once more. "We are the Thieves and we are stealing back freedom!" she called from the top of her lungs.

The people below erupted in a mixture of praise and derision, coming alive as she stood there, arms raised. The councillor was barking orders to the soldiers in the streets and whomever hadn't reached Orangecloak's previous position were doing anything they could to get free of the tightly packed throng. At first, she thought that the Master of Blades had would surely be advancing on her and she scanned the area to the left of the jewellery store for him. Much to Orangecloak's surprise, she followed the trail all the way back to the street where Tryst Reine had been, finding him standing in exactly the same spot.

Coquarro grabbed her by the arm and began to haul her away as soldiers began piling onto the roof of the stall below them. "Red, we must leave with haste if we are to get out of this alive and free," he advised her.

"Did you see him?" Orangecloak asked as they began running. "Tryst Reine was there."

"Then we should run even faster, Red," Coquarro cautioned, with his voice full of urgency, yet still somehow calm and measured. "I do not want to face him this day."

The guards shouted at them from below to stay put

and surrender.

Given that Orangecloak and Coquarro had no intention of doing any such thing, they broke into a run.

They leapt from one roof to the next several times across the narrow gaps. The fifth roof they came to was further and lower and required a longer jump and a rolling landing. The next building was too high to leap to, but a balcony with an open door was at the same elevation as they and the two made for it. An old man was seated inside at a small table, fanning himself in the sultry heat. Orangecloak apologised for the intrusion and asked if there was another way out of the apartment. Despite his initial shock, he nodded and pointed to the right of where they came in to a long, open window.

Coquarro looked out through it and came back with a scowl on his face. "That's a one way trip to the alley below. We're not looking to die just yet."

"No, don't go out the window. Look up, young one," the man told them.

Orangecloak looked above Coquarro's head. "There's a hatch!" she pointed out to Coquarro, leaving him to open it while turning back to the old man. "I'm sorry again for barging in. Thank you for all your help."

"Least I can do. Steal back freedom, young ones!" he called out to them as they climbed the sliding ladder to the roof above. Coquarro pulled it shut behind him and they took off southward once more.

Guards were climbing onto the roofs wherever they could find ladders and were trying their best to catch up to the Thieves. "Stop at once!" one called from nearby to the left while pulling a pistol from his belt. When neither

Orangecloak nor Coquarro complied, he fired his lone shot, fortunately missing them both.

For a second, she turned and looked back at him and all about, seeing only bluecoats clambering up after them. *No sign of him. If he did give pursuit he's not chasing us from up here,* Orangecloak told herself.

"Come on, Red, not too far now!" Coquarro shouted at her when he finally noticed that she wasn't beside him any longer.

They took off again, running and jumping two more roofs until they were at the catwalk that allowed the guards direct access from the recruitment centre to the rooftops.

The rickety, wooden footbridge shook unsteadily beneath their feet as they made their way, crossing over a wide, busy street filled with people, horses, and carriages below.

Behind the tall spire that stretched high enough to peek atop the city walls, they found Merion and Myles, crouched low and waiting. Along with the apparel she was already wearing to match Orangecloak, Merion had tied a linen replica of the signature cloak across her shoulders. It wasn't an exact copy of the famous orange cloak, but served more than ably to make Merion an excellent decoy.

As much as Orangecloak would have like to, there was no time to stop for a rest. As they had done many times before, Coquarro switched places with Myles without a word and the two teams bolted in opposite directions out of hiding.

The guards, having caught up with their targets, were crossing the rickety, wooden overpass one man at a time when the four Thieves burst forth from behind the spire. Orangecloak estimated there to be a dozen or so in total, some atop the same roof as the Thieves, but most waiting to cross.

As they caught sight of the two pairs of runners, every man among them seemed to have a different idea of which one to pursue. They cursed and shouted over one another and in trying to decide which redheaded, orange-cloaked woman was the real one, had stalled in their tracks.

When Orangecloak looked over her shoulder again, she saw that roughly half of the guards that had crossed the rickety catwalk were now giving chase of her and Myles. The other half, she suspected, were hot on the trail of Merion and Coquarro.

This leg of the escape was more suited to Myles, who was far more agile and dexterous than Coquarro. The route they had mapped out led them downhill, but the jumps between buildings were longer and the drops higher than they had been.

It was no secret that this sort of risky, dangerous behaviour was commonplace for the Thieves, and to Coquarro's credit he was passably good at the acrobatic feats. For Myles though, it was as if he was bred for it. The man saw nothing in his path as an insurmountable obstacle and for as long as Orangecloak had known him, she still found herself barely able to keep up.

Finally, after an exhausting sprint, the two of them came to the waterfront area. With a wide, open street below, the only way left to them was down. In a flash Myles had vaulted over the rear of the building, grabbing the roof's lip as he turned in mid-air and hanging from the side. Orangecloak followed suit and the two began jumping back and forth between it and the previous building they had leapt from, getting closer to the ground with every timed jump. They touched down safely and ducked inside the first unlocked door they found, leaving the door open a crack to listen for their pursuers.

"They're gone!" one guard shouted from somewhere overhead.

Another made the jump to the building facing the waterfront street and after a tense few minutes returned to his comrades. "I'm not seeing any immediate way down, but it's the only way they could have gone unless they climbed the town walls."

"The gods be damned!" a voice shouted that Orangecloak could only assume to belong to that of the highest ranking guard among the bunch. "Hurry up and let's find a way down. There should be a ladder a few houses back we can use. Detain every red haired woman you see, no exceptions. If we've lost sight of her, she might already be in disguise."

Orangecloak exhaled at last and let her body relax. "That should give us a few minutes. Let's get out of here and make sure we put as much distance between us and them as we can." Ever so casually, she began tying back her hair into a tight tail to hide it away. For the first time since leaving the former woodshed of Coramae's family, Orangecloak actually felt calm and as she worked on the ponytail, she idly asked Myles, "Where did we end up to anyhow?"

"As to that…" Myles began to say, trailing off as he looked beyond where they had been huddled beside the door.

It was at that moment that she felt many eyes upon her, all at once. Slowly, Orangecloak turned in the direction Myles was facing and looked across a tavern full of patrons, all male and most of them at least a decade older than she and Myles. The pair of Thieves had just so happened to slip inside the rear delivery door of the establishment. Though the alcove the door rested in was darkened, it was directly beside the bar and in plain sight of everyone within.

The recognition on the faces of the men sitting shoulder to shoulder was plain to see. There was no way for Orangecloak to feasibly deny who she was, especially in light of the fact that she was still wearing the cloak she was named for. The only thing left to wonder was if these men saw her as a friend or a foe.

In an effort to gauge as much, Orangecloak took a single, careful step forward, her hands out with her palms raised upward. "Gentlemen, I apologise for disturbing you," she said as a peace offering. "We mean no trouble and we'll be leaving as quickly as we came."

Not one of them made a move to answer her, though their stares remained fixed. She glanced to Myles, who was clearly feeling every bit as nervous as she and they began to slowly back away towards the rear door.

A big, gruff looking fellow with hairy arms, a thick beard, a fading hairline and a menacing face began to advance on them. Given that he was wearing an apron, Orangecloak guessed he was the barkeeper and she was about to apologise to him once more when he reached up high to a shelf unseen.

Myles began to work the latch on the door and Orangecloak was ready to make a bolt for it when the barkeep called out to them, "Wait just a moment, you two."

They froze in place, Orangecloak's heart beating ferociously in her chest.

The keeper's hand came away from the shelf and in it was an old, floppy, felt hat. He beat a layer of dust off it with his other hand and plopped it down on Orangecloak's head. "That should help to keep your hair covered," he said sternly, but not unkindly. "No one here wants to go to Biddenhurst on your account, miss, so I suggest you take off that cloak before you go so that no one sees it. Then scurry out that back door and make sure none of the guards see you and want to come sniffing about. Do we have a deal?"

"Yes, of course, thank you," Orangecloak answered with a bow. She undid her own cloak, rolled it quickly around an arm and stuffed it into Myles' satchel. The brown, linen cloak Myles had been wearing was then given to Orangecloak to further conceal her clothing, which the guards would most certainly be on the lookout for. With a last nod, the pair turned back to the door, checked that the alley was clear and left hastily.

The main road running along the waterfront was a hive of activity and there certainly was a heavy presence of guards about, but none seemed the slightest bit interested in Orangecloak, Myles, or the pursuit of the Thieves. The two strode amongst the townsfolk casually, trying to act as though they belonged and saw no eyes being cast their way.

As Orangecloak got a peek in the general direction that the crowd were focused she realised why the guards were so preoccupied. "I'll have to give Lazlo full credit for that distraction he devised. It worked far better than I could have imagined," she said to Myles in a low voice.

The majority of the guards had been dispatched to the pier and were still working to quell the brawl that Lazlo and his unit had instigated there. Without that, Orangecloak had no doubt that there would be far more men searching for her.

A racket to her left caught her attention and Orangecloak glanced to find the guards that had been chasing her and Myles across the rooftops were now on the ground and searching noisily through everything they saw. "Our pursuers are one street over," she informed Myles. "Just keep walking casually and they shouldn't be too interested in us."

By mid-afternoon the two had walked unbothered along the south side of Aquas Bay. As they went, the city fell away to a smattering of modest homes. Local fishermen who docked their skiffs and dories in the many coves that dotted this side of the naval port owned everything here. It was as ideal a location as one could get in the Southlands, Orangecloak knew. They were offered the protection of the Aquas Bay's imposing walls without the noise and bluster of the city. At the end of the long wall, the duo found the old lighthouse tower. There was always a keeper on duty and no less than two guards to keep watch, but passing beyond them unnoticed was nothing Orangecloak was ever bothered by.

The tower was built centuries before, atop a cliff overlooking the ocean. In that long time those cliffs had been eaten away by the rough seas that roared through in the early autumn nearly every year. It had been told to Orangecloak that from the sea, the tower looked like it might well tumble to the rocks below at a moment's notice. The former basement was left open and exposed to the elements and was quite nearly rotted away, but enough remained that it made for a fairly dangerous, albeit traversable passageway to the other side of the wall.

For Orangecloak and Myles, it was a relatively easy descent over the rock face. Far below lay jagged rocks and crashing waves, but Orangecloak knew better than to look at them and she kept her focus solely on her own climbing. Finally, her foot touched lumber and she dared to look below for the first time, finding herself on a support beam of the tower's ruined cellar. She put her stomach to the rock wall and began shimmying along the beam until she came to an alcove that allowed for a little more room to manoeuvre. Myles was following close behind and they continued along the wall, stomachs against its smooth surface, feet shuffling along another beam. The climb out to the gulch was far easier than the descent and within no time they were on the other side of the city walls once more.

Ahead lay the old forest far away from the city centre that had been allowed to creep its way right into the shadow of the ancient lighthouse.

Myles waited until they were beneath the canopy of the trees before he asked the burning question: "How did the protest go?"

At first she deigned to answer, letting herself breathe deep of the forest air and relax. Overhead the songbirds chirped and sang sweetly and gave Orangecloak an overwhelming sense of calm. Her stride slowed to a saunter and she undid both her hair ribbon and Myles' cloak. It was then she remembered the hat and took it off as well, opting to carry it in both hands and use it as a fan. "It went well, I thought," she answered Myles just as he was growing even more impatient. "A councillor happened to be in the market, I think it was Councillor Havellan. He got riled up by the things I said and I think I answered his jeering quite well."

"That's not all, is it?" Myles asked concernedly. "I had to take off and get to Merion's location midway through, I missed much of your speech. Pray tell, what happened?"

"You were right, Myles. Tryst Reine did show up," Orangecloak finally admitted.

His eyes went wide in surprise and he began glancing over his shoulder, as if he was expecting to be followed. "By the gods, I had no idea that the Master of Blades saw you. Why didn't you tell me this sooner?"

She shook her head slowly, reflecting back on the sight of him. "That's the thing, Myles. He didn't make a move to capture me. All the Master of Blades did was stand in the crowd with his arms folded, listening and watching. Even when Coquarro and I were making our escape, I looked back and there he was, still in the exact same spot."

That didn't seem to satisfy Myles and he continued to look all about. "Damn him, I bet he followed us. I should double back to the lighthouse and try to get him while he's climbing the rocks. It might be the only chance to take him unawares."

"Tryst Reine is not coming after us, Myles," Orangecloak said reassuringly. "He watched me leave and made no effort to do anything. I don't know why, but I can tell you that we're alive now for only one reason."

"And what do you think that is?" Myles asked.

Orangecloak straightened, looking him in the eye. "Tryst Reine had no desire to arrest us."

Ali House

Alison House is an Award-Winning, Bestselling author, a playwright, a traveler, and a reader.

A native Newfoundlander, House is a graduate of the Fine Arts program at Sir Wilfred Grenfell College (MUN). She currently resides in Halifax, Nova Scotia, where she works in arts administration and spends more time than a person should in and around theaters.

House won the December 2018 Kit Sora Prize, which celebrates authors throughout Canada. Her short fiction has appeared in every issue of the *From the Rock* anthology series, as well as *Bluenose Paradox* and the *Kit Sora Artobiography*.

Her novels include *The Six Elemental* and *The Fifth Queen*.

Twenty-One

"Wake up! It's almost midnight!"

Naydir reluctantly opened his eyes. It was too dark to see anything so he shut them again. He had been deep asleep, dreaming of a beach – not the grainy beach they used to visit in Cambria, but a strange soft white sanded beach, with green water and blue sky going on forever and ever. If he went back to sleep, maybe he could find the dream again…

"Stay awake!" His sister shook him roughly, refusing to let him fall asleep again.

"I'm up." He yawned and pulled himself into a sitting position. He only had himself to blame for this rude awakening. After all, it had been his decision to get a few hours of sleep instead of staying up all night, as his sister had done. It was his personal opinion that she was making a big deal out of nothing, but that was kind of her style.

Moonlight streamed in through the window of their dorm room, and when his eyes adjusted to the darkness he was able to see the determination on his sister's face. She'd been waiting for this day for a long time, and she wasn't going to let a pathetic bodily need like sleep ruir it.

As they waited for midnight, they sat side by side on the floor of their room, backs resting against Zenyth's bed. The other trainees in the Peacekeeper Academy were asleep, so it was oddly quiet. Normally there would be people running to and from training or practicing in the hallways. Even during final exams, the building was never this silent or still.

Naydir yawned and his sister elbowed him sharply. He gave her an exhausted look, but she didn't apologize. They stared silently at the glowing numerals of the wall clock. Finally the time moved from 11:59pm to 12:00am. Zenyth took in a deep breath and let it out slowly.

"So, anything happening?" he asked.

Her eyes widened. "I think I finally understand advanced biometrics!"

"Be serious, Z."

"I got nothing. You?"

"Nothing."

They sat silently for another minute. It was now 12:01am on January 17, 695 years after the Last World War.

Zenyth had been planning this night for the past 16 years and, although she'd accounted for a few different variables, her plan always included something happening exactly at the stroke of midnight.

"I told you that it wouldn't happen right away," he couldn't help saying as he stifled another yawn.

"But it could have."

"Are we really going to sit here and watch the clock all night?"

"Why? We don't have to train tomorrow. We've got a pass."

"I feel stupid."

"It's only been one – I mean, two minutes."

"We can't stay awake for twenty-four hours, Z."

"But what if it happens while we're asleep?" she protested. "What if we sleep through it? We might not get another chance!"

He yawned. "If it happens while we're asleep then we'll probably wake up."

"You don't know that we will."

"You don't know that we won't."

They stared at each other, wondering who would give in first. They both knew that it would probably be Naydir. This wasn't the first time they'd disagreed on something and it wouldn't be the last. One of the worst things about being a twin was that everyone expected the two of you to be exactly the same. Every time the two of them disagreed it was as though they were letting down nature itself.

It didn't help that they looked exactly alike, with the same tall, thin build and round face with sharp features. The only difference was that Naydir was male and Zenyth was female, but even that didn't provide much of a contrast. She would have looked more feminine if she grew out her dark hair instead of wearing it short like her brother, but it was more practical for a peacekeeper to have hair that wouldn't get in the way. Besides, she had no problem with the way she looked, so everyone else could just get over it.

At first glance, it was difficult to figure out who was who, but there was no mistaking Zenyth once she opened her mouth. She was brasher and more opinionated than her brother. Naydir was more diplomatic and practical, and thought about what he was going to say before he said it. They were different, but it was more complimentary than polarizing. Of course they fought, and sometimes they would stay angry at each other for days before finally reconciling or giving in, but they never forgot that they were family.

"Do you think it'll happen at the same time?" Zenyth asked.

He shrugged. "I don't know. I mean, we were born four minutes apart. Maybe it'll happen like that."

"You just want to be first."

"Who wouldn't?" He glanced at the clock, which was now displaying the time as 12:05am. "You know, we weren't born until 10am."

"I'm not going to sleep."

"There's no rule that says–"

"And there's no rule that doesn't."

They stared at each other again. Even with the sparse illumination Naydir could tell that his sister was disappointed in him.

Today was their 21st birthday and it was a very important day. Today they would each receive a vision and make the choice to accept the responsibilities of an element or not. They had no idea when the vision would happen or which one of the six elements it would be – they only knew that it would happen sometime today.

Scientists had been trying to come up with a formula to predict the visions for decades, but tests were still inconclusive. Every time they thought that they had worked it out, they would receive data which did not conform and be sent back to square one. It was as if every Elemental's EDNA was in constant flux until the exact moment of the vision. It was almost as infuriating for them as independent genes.

Naydir had often thought about what it would be like to accept an element. His preference was either earth or electricity. Those elements would be useful, especially when it came to dealing with delinquents. Zenyth, he knew from experience, wanted fire or electricity. He wondered if they would get the same element or different.

There was a chance that they would not have a vision, that they would have no choice and remain neutral, and that chance was why Zenyth refused to go to sleep. She didn't want to be one of the small fraction of Elementals without an element. Nobody knew why some people remained neutral, but scientists were still trying to figure it out – along with all the other anomalies that lay within the Elemental EDNA. It would be disappointing to have no choice, but Naydir knew that there was nothing he could do about it. Besides, he was certain that if they were meant to have a vision then they would have one. He couldn't explain this feeling to his sister. It was just a feeling, and Zenyth didn't care much about feelings.

"Did it happen?" she asked.

Naydir broke out of his thoughts. "What?"

"Did you get it?"

"No."

"Damn. You were spaced out for so long that I thought it happened."

"I was just thinking."

"About what?"

He shrugged.

"Then stop thinking. You're making it difficult for me to tell what's going on."

"I'm not going to talk to you for twenty-four hours straight."

"Twenty-three hours and forty-seven minutes," she corrected.

"Z," he sighed, "I'm going to sleep. I don't want to spend the night sitting here not talking and not thinking."

"No."

"You can't forbid me from going to bed."

"No, but I can be annoying and keep you up all night."

"Zenyth..."

She let out a frustrated growl. "But what if you miss it? It would be horrible for only one of us to get a vision. Besides, I want to share the experience with you, you scorch-mark."

Naydir laughed. His sister could be so sentimental sometimes. "I appreciate the love, but I don't think I'll miss anything if I go to sleep."

"You might."

"And I might not."

Zenyth was silent. He had a feeling that this time his sister would be the one to cave.

"Fine, you can sleep. Just don't go crying to me if you don't get a vision and have to spend the rest of your life watching me do cool stuff while you forever live with your silent regrets."

He smiled and hugged her. "Thank you. I hope you'll take my advice and not stay up all night."

"I guarantee nothing."

He stood up and pulled back the sheets on his bed, ready to go back to that warm, sandy beach. Suddenly his sight went completely black. He saw a vision of the earth cracking open into a giant chasm. Sand and rocks broke apart, falling inward as the chasm grew larger and larger. The vision faded into black and Naydir knew what he had to do.

When he opened his eyes, the room was suddenly bright. He quickly shut his eyes, trying to block out the brightness, but everything was red behind his eyelids.

"What happened?" Zenyth asked eagerly. She'd tried to get his attention, and when he didn't speak to her, she'd turned on the lights. He had been standing by his bed, motionless for almost a minute. "Did you get one? Did you get a vision?"

He nodded. Now that he had time to adjust to the lights, he could see the joy on his sister's face.

"What was it?"

He pulled up the left leg of his pants. Above his ankle was a dark brown square, about an inch tall.

"Earth?! That's great!" Zenyth hugged him. "Did it hurt?"

"It felt like pins and needles, but not bad."

The Tattoo happened after acceptance and it was a mark that all element-wielding Elementals bore. If someone's claim about an element was tested, they had to be willing to show the mark to prove it. Naydir was really glad that it wasn't anywhere embarrassing.

"I'm not sure how I feel about earth," she remarked, mostly to herself. "It's not as cool as electricity or fire, but it's better than nothing." She sat back down on the floor, across from him. "I wonder when I'm going to get my vision. Maybe four minutes from now?"

"I don't know," he replied. "I guess we'll have to wait and see."

Even before he opened his eyes, Naydir could feel the ache in his muscles. He was leaning back against the bed, his legs crossed and head to one side. He couldn't remember falling asleep, but it had been for long enough that there was a serious crick in his neck. He was going to feel sore today.

When he looked across the room he saw his sister sitting across from him, staring at the wall clock with tired, red eyes. The time was 8:27am.

"Have you been up all this time?" he asked, rising stiffly to his feet.

"Maybe."

"...Did it happen?"

She didn't reply.

He wasn't sure what to say. "Well, you probably could have gone to sleep after all."

"Shut up."

Her tone was angry, but he could see the slightest hint of amusement on her face.

"Breakfast?" he asked, stretching out his sore muscles. "I'll watch over you if you space out."

"I suppose."

They changed clothes and headed towards the cafeteria. Breakfast was served until 9am for the recruits, so there was still time for them to eat. They passed by a few other recruits, mostly heading in the opposite direction.

"Happy birthday!"

They turned around and saw Todd jogging up to them. He was shorter and broader than the twins, so the double-hug he gave them was delightfully awkward. Naydir and Zenyth exchanged an amused look over Todd's light blue hair. Their friend would always choose the most awkward option when presented with a choice.

"Thanks," Naydir said. "Are you heading to the cafeteria?"

"Of course – just had to find you two first. So..." Todd continued, his violet eyes sparkling. "Did it happen yet?"

Naydir looked at Zenyth, who was frowning again. He didn't want to leave her out by saying that his vision had come but not hers. She rolled her eyes, giving him permission to speak.

"I had mine last night," Naydir said.

"Congratulations! What Element?"

"Earth."

"Nice." Todd looked at Zenyth. "How about you? Earth, too?"

Zenyth ignored Todd and continued walking.

"She didn't get hers yet," Naydir said quietly.

"Oh... Sorry, I shouldn't have said anything."

"Don't worry about it. I'm sure it'll happen soon. She's just upset because she thought that she'd get hers first."

Todd promised not to mention it again, but as they walked into the cafeteria they realized that Todd wasn't the only problem. As Zenyth walked through the room, people called out to wish her a happy birthday and to inquire about the vision. She was ignoring everyone, but Naydir could practically see the black cloud hanging over her head. He had to get to her quickly and do some damage control.

"I'm guessing someone didn't have a vision yet," a loud voice boomed throughout the cafeteria.

Naydir sighed. It was Iain, Zenyth's arch-enemy. It was weird that Zenyth called him that, but Naydir had to admit that whenever anything went wrong for her, Iain was there.

"The day's still young," Naydir countered. "There's plenty of time."

"Is there?" another voice chimed in. "By my calculations there's less than two-thirds of the day left."

Rinn was Iain's best friend and the two were almost inseparable. Her eyes were a dark brown instead of Iain's orange, but they both had the same light grey hair. Everyone suspected that they dyed their hair so that they'd match, but the two of them insisted that it was natural.

"Just go away," Naydir said firmly. He could see the tension in his sister's body and knew that she could resort to violence at any minute.

Rinn laughed. "Why would I want to go away? Zenyth is so utterly frustrated and..." She paused and a wicked smile crossed her face.

Naydir wished that a piano would fall on her head, or a safe, or a tonne of cabbages, but no such luck.

"Your brother got his vision and you didn't!" Rinn exclaimed. "How amazing!"

Iain burst out laughing. "Congratulations on being a dud!"

Naydir rarely lost his temper, but now was one of those moments when he was ready to beat his sister to the punch. "Leave her alone," he threatened, stepping towards them.

Rinn gave one last laugh and walked away. Iain blew Zenyth a kiss before falling into step beside her.

"Zenyth," Naydir began gently, turning to her, "don't let what they said get to you. I'm sure you'll get your vision soon."

"Don't you have training to go to?" she asked icily.

"I'm exempt. It's our birthday."

"You got your vision, so you can go."

"But didn't you want-"

"I want you to go to training. There's no reason the two of us should miss out." Zenyth stormed out of the cafeteria.

Todd shrugged. "She's got a point."

"Yeah. That's what has me worried."

In the end, Naydir went to his classes. He quietly talked to his instructors about Zenyth not getting her vision yet, but the secrecy was pointless. Iain and Rinn were already spreading word about Zenyth's inactivity. Never mind that the day wasn't over yet and anything could happen. When Zenyth got her vision, he knew that she was going to make Iain and Rinn suffer.

At lunch he kept an eye out for his sister, but she never showed. Before he went back to training, he took a quick trip to their room, grabbing some fruit to take to her since he was certain that she wasn't eating. When he opened the door, she was sitting on her bed, staring off into space.

"Nothing yet?"

"Surprise, surprise," she said vacantly. "Maybe I am a dud."

"Don't think that. There's still half a day left."

"You got yours right away."

"That doesn't mean anything, Z. There are a lot of twins who get their visions at different times." He sighed. "Have you eaten anything today?"

She didn't respond.

"I brought you some fruit, but the cafeteria's still open if you want real food."

"Whatever."

When training was over, Naydir headed to supper with the rest of his class. He looked around for Zenyth again, but she wasn't there. Instead of sitting down, he left the cafeteria and headed straight to his room.

"This has got to stop," he said as he burst into the room. Zenyth was still on her bed, just like before, and the fruit he'd left untouched. He wouldn't have been surprised if she hadn't moved an inch since he last saw her.

She gave a bitter laugh. "What's got to stop? Nothing's happening – which, I might add, is entirely the problem."

"Snap out of it. You can't lock yourself in a room for the rest of your life."

"It's worked so far. No Iain, no Rinn..."

"There's still time."

"Is there time for you to shut up?" she muttered.

Naydir sat down next to her. "So what if you don't get a vision? Plenty of people don't have elements."

"And most of them are duds or stupid, jerky Humanists."

"I'd rather be a dud than a Humanist. Besides, only jerks refer to vision-less people as duds," he remarked.

"Well, it's an appropriate term, because I feel exactly like a dud right now."

Naydir had no idea what to say to her to make her feel better. "How about I get us some food before supper ends?"

Zenyth muttered something that he wasn't sure he wanted to make out.

When he left the room, he ran into Todd.

"What's going on?" Todd asked, concerned.

"She thinks she's a dud."

"So what if she is? You don't need an element to be a peacekeeper."

"It helps."

"Okay, fine it helps. But you still don't need one. I mean, my birthday's not for two months. What if I turn out to be a dud? It won't be the end of my world."

"Yeah, but you know Zenyth. She's been waiting for this forever."

Todd frowned. "There's still time. She could still get a vision."

Naydir sighed. "I hope so. I don't know what to do if she doesn't."

Naydir brought back a tray of food from the cafeteria. He'd finished his supper quickly, but Zenyth's plate remained on her desk, untouched. Currently he was torn between demanding that his sister eat something and offering to eat it for her.

They sat in silence for hours. She refused to talk. He tried reading, but nothing held his attention. Normally he liked a bit of silence, but Zenyth's unmovable attitude was driving him crazy. He'd rather be in the training room, testing his new abilities some more, but he couldn't leave her like this.

"Z," he finally said, "it's 10:14. You've been up for almost 40 hours. Go to bed."

"No."

"If it's meant to be, it will be."

She swore and put her head in her hands. "I don't care if it's meant to be. I don't care if it's fated that I don't get a vision. I want one and I can't understand why it's not happening!"

"It's going to be okay."

"No, it's not!"

He didn't understand why she was reacting this way. "Why does this matter so much to you?" he asked.

She looked up at him. "Because you got a vision! When I pictured this night, I entertained the slim possibility that we might not get a vision, but never in my life did I think that only one of us would get an element! You can't tell me that it wouldn't bother you if I had a vision and you didn't."

"It might not."

"It would! We've shared every major experience – our birthdays, our driver's tests, getting accepted into the police academy. But this – this whole thing about me not getting a vision – that isn't something that I can share with you. You don't know what it's like to have to live the rest of your life as a dud. And I won't know what it's like to have an element."

"So what? It's not like we'll suddenly stop being twins."

"But it might be the beginning of the end. This might be the day where we start drifting away from one another. I mean, we're not exactly identical when it comes to personality. What if this drives a wedge between us?"

He shook his head. "We won't let that happen."

She looked down at her hands. "Maybe it wouldn't happen if it was you without an element, but I might let it. I can admit I'm not a big enough person to not let it get between us."

"Z..."

"There's nothing you can do to help. Just be quiet."

He walked over and sat down next to her. "If I could give you my element, I would."

"I know, and that makes me feel even worse."

He was quiet for a few seconds. "I know that we look identical, but we've always been very different people. I think it's what makes us a great team. This is just one more difference."

"Yeah, well it's one that I didn't sign up for."

"Zenyth–"

"I don't want to talk about this anymore." She turned away from him. "I'm going to go to bed. Might as well get this stupid day over with."

He wished that there were something he could do for his sister. If he could have shared his element with her or given it up so that they'd both be element-less he would have, but it was impossible.

Naydir walked over to his bed and turned down the sheets. When he looked back at his sister, he saw that she hadn't moved. For a moment he'd thought that she was actually going to sleep, but chances were she'd stay awake until midnight. He wondered if she'd ever sleep again.

"You should go to bed," he said.

No reply.

"Z, you should get some sleep."

When there was still no reply, he walked over to her. She was staring off into space, looking at nothing in particular. Naydir looked at the wall clock; it was10:34pm.

"Zenyth?"

She jumped, as if she'd just woken up. A look of relief crossed her face and a wide smile broke out.

His mouth dropped open. "You got a vision?"

She nodded.

"What element? Earth, like me?"

She shook her head and pulled up the right leg of her pants. On her ankle was a tattoo the same size as her brother's, but hers was of two wavy blue lines.

It was fitting, really. Her element was the opposite of his.

Air.

Afterword
Erin Vance

For the last seven years, as I've made my daily trek from my house into the city, I am always taken by surprise at the sign proclaiming Sci Fi on the Rock's return. *Oh! It's back again. I've got to remember to go this year.* Then, likely like most of you people, I forget all about it until I see the sign again the next day. And the next day. Until all of a sudden, the weekend is here, and I forgot to book it off work. Again.

As you can probably tell, unlike most of the other contributors to this anthology, I have never been a vendor at Sci Fi on the Rock. I've only ever experienced the convention as an attendee– and not even as a truly inspired attendee. I've never been to a panel (although a couple have caught my interest), I've never dressed up past a geeky T-shirt I would wear around the mall, and I've never spoken to one of the many, *many* vendors that gather there. In fact, I've always kept my head down, a limited amount of cash on hand, and a polite smile on my face for when authors try to catch my eye (I think it was Scott Bartlett last year; I'm sorry for ignoring you, dude. I now have new appreciation of your side of the table). I go because, for me, Sci Fi on the Rock is less of an adventure and weekend of freedom, and more of a sign that spring is coming and a chance to people-watch.

I haven't gone every year; in fact, I think I've only gone three or four times. I've bought an Eevee necklace (because those are my initials), a Captain America T-shirt, and a couple of things for my siblings. Mostly, I gawk at all the people around me, the people that know so much more about Science Fiction, Fantasy, and all other things geeky than I do. As I watch, I find myself absorbed into the sense of community that fills the rooms and halls. At Sci Fi on the Rock, it doesn't matter how much of a geek or a nerd you are. Maybe you're a person who's only interested in a couple of things; maybe you love every little aspect of the convention. Either way, you are welcomed to enjoy the company of others just like you: people who are passionate about something. And it's that shared sense of passion that makes Sci Fi on the Rock such an amazing experience.

We hope that we've captured that sense of passion and community within this anthology. Just as every person – attendee and vendor – is unique, so too are these authors and their stories. Just as the convention welcomes you to share in its geekery, so do these authors welcome you into their world of fiction, no matter the genre. While some of them explore humanity in all its forms, some are just offering an escape from the crazy, cynical world we live in.

So, thank you for sharing in our passions, and may you continue to develop your own. Maybe this year at Sci Fi, you can find a way to grow – some of you might follow my example and evolve from a attendee to a vendor (no Moonstone required; although a friendship level certainly helps)! Enjoy the little things in life, my friends, and remember that they're what make life worthwhile.

God bless,
Erin Vance
Editor

ON THE COVER

This year's amazing photo and CGI composite cover artwork was shot and designed by Kyle Callahan of Kyle Callahan Photography, who does the astonishing forced-perspective science-fiction-themed pieces of artwork that have been a staple of Sci-Fi on the Rock for several years.

Kyle sought to bring an iconic Newfoundland image -- jellybean houses with the Narrows and Signal Hill in the background -- and add classic sci-fi flare to it with a retro-designed robot straight from the 60s pulp magazines attacking the city.

Engen Books thanks Kyle for helping out and look forward to working with him in the future! Check out his spectacular work at www.KyleCallahan.ca

Did you enjoy Scott Bartlett's work on page 67? See what else he has in store!

Titles by Scott Bartlett

Royal Flush

Taking Stock

Finished with Life but Unable to Die

Flight or Fight

You can find out what becomes of Carl Intoever in *Flight or Fight*, which is available for download in its entirety on any reading device. Visit ScottPlots.com for more information.

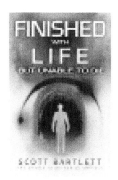

If you enjoyed the Prologue to *Whitecoat* from page 7, you're in luck: with over 30 titles spread over four different long-running series, Kenneth Tam has something for everyone! *Whitecoat* as its sequels are available in print and online now!

THE CHAMPIONS OF 1940
WHITECOAT
KENNETH TAM

Since 1881, Britain, Canada and the United States have been colonizing another planet. Now it's 1940, and tensions between the world's Empires are mounting because the English-speaking nations enjoy exclusive control over a uniquely powerful resource: genetically-enhanced humans known as 'Champions'. Lady Alex Smith is the newest Champion, and her best friend Stephanie Shylock has joined the British Army so they can work together. Along with Sergeant Mike Strong, a veteran soldier with a colorful reputation, these two must follow in the footsteps of their famous parents, and save the world... perhaps both worlds.

ICEBERG PUBLISHING

As impossible as it sounds, *Super Galactic Space Explorers* is even more entertaining in comic book form!

The light hearted space-adventure written by co-creator Jay Paulin with art by co-creator Ariel Marsh brings a fresh take to the Space Opera format by adding the most popular thing on the internet: CATS!

Mixing high-energy, a crisp all-ages writing style, clean art and a witty premise, *Super Galactic Space* Explorers is the most can't-miss coming to come out of Canada in 40 years!

Visit Ink'd Well Comics today and pick up *A Call to Paws* and *Royal Pain* today! Volume Three coming soon!

art by Ariel Marsh

An adventurous cat
and her allies face
off against evildoers
across the galaxy.

The Super Galactic
Space Explorers, along
with their allies, must
act quickly to save the
galaxy from the evil
Queen Kitkat.

SCI-FI FROM THE ROCK

A COLLECTION OF SHORT STORIES
EDITED BY ERIN VANCE & ELLEN CURTIS

Nineteen short stories written by an eclectic mix of some of the best science-fiction and fantasy authors in Atlantic Canada, some of them award-winning veterans and some of them new to the craft for the first time.

Edited by English Honours Graduate and Professional Editor Erin Vance and veteran science-fiction author Ellen Louise Curtis, this collection features the heartfelt, creatively charged, astonishing fiction that showcases the talent and charm Atlantic Canada has to offer.

Featuring the work of Kenneth Tam, Scott Bartlett, Jay Paulin, Ali House, Matthew Daniels & many more!

Printed in Great Britain
by Amazon